A Note from Lucy Daniels

Dear readers,

I'm so excited that Hodder Children's Books is publishing your favourite titles as Animal Ark Classics. I can't believe it's ten years since Mandy and James had their first adventure. I've written so many stories about them they feel like real friends to me now and it's been such fun thinking up new stories for them both.

I know from your letters how much you enjoy sharing their love of animals. As you can tell, I'm a huge fan of animals myself, and can't imagine a day when I will ever want to stop writing about them.

Happy reading!

Very best wishes,

Lucy

LUCY DANIELS

ANIMAL ARK™
CLASSICS

KOALAS IN A CRISIS

Hodder
Children's
Books

A division of Hodder Headline Limited

Special thanks to Jenny Oldfield.
Thanks also to veterinarian Bairbre O'Malley for reviewing the
veterinary information contained in this book.

Animal Ark is a trademark of Working Partners Limited
Copyright © 1996 Working Partners Limited
Created by Working Partners Limited, London W6 0QT
Original series created by Ben M. Baglio

First published in Great Britain in 1996
by Hodder Children's Books

This edition published in 2005

For more information about Animal Ark, please contact
www.animalark.co.uk

2 4 6 8 10 9 7 5 3 1

A Catalogue record for this book is available from the British Library

ISBN 0 340 88164 X

Typeset in Baskerville by Avon DataSet Ltd,
Bidford-on-Avon, Warwickshire

Printed and bound in Great Britain by
Clays Ltd, St Ives plc

The paper and board used in this paperback by Hodder Children's
Books are natural recyclable products made from wood grown in
sustainable forests. The manufacturing processes conform to the
environmental regulations of the country of origin.

Hodder Children's Books
a division of Hodder Headline Limited
338 Euston Road
London NW1 3BH

One

'Mandy, come and look at this!' Adam Hope called from the creek behind Mitchell Gap. The sun was going down; a kookaburra called from the high gum trees.

Mandy lifted her feet out of the clear blue water of their outdoor pool. She ran barefoot across the yard. Her dad sounded excited. 'Where are you?' She searched up and down the side of the stream.

'Shh! Over here.' Mr Hope crouched over the bank. He hung on to a tree branch and peered into the deep, clear water. He didn't look like a man who'd just flown across the world from England and driven six hundred kilometres from

Sydney, Australia, to Eurabbie Bay. He looked fresh and eager in his shorts and T-shirt, his bearded face alive with curiosity.

Mandy leaped across the creek. 'What, Dad? What?' She stared underwater, but she couldn't see anything.

'It is!' he cried. 'I'm sure it is!'

Mandy went down on all fours on to the red, sandy earth. 'I can't see a thing!'

'Yes, look. There!' He stabbed his finger towards the water and hissed.

And there, gliding through the reeds and rocks of the river-bed, was the strangest creature Mandy had ever set eyes on. Shaped like a grey barrel, with a tail like a beaver and a bill like a duck, it paddled with its webbed feet and snouted in the mud for worms. Mandy glanced up at her dad. 'Is it a platypus?'

He nodded. 'It sure is.' He gazed at the submerged creature's every move.

Mandy took a deep breath. This was her very first day in Australia, and she'd already seen one of its rare wonders. She had read that the platypus would only come out in the evening, after a day tucked snug inside its burrow.

'Greedy little tyke!' Mr Hope grinned as the

platypus snouted round for more worms and crayfish.

'It's eating the mud!' They watched it suck and sieve the murky water through its bill. 'Can't it see what it's picking up?' Mandy asked.

'Not underwater.' Adam Hope got his nose almost to water level. His tree branch creaked and bent. 'Look, it has a flap of skin that comes down over its ears and eyes. It has to feel its way with its bill!'

Mandy felt tremendous, like the first person ever to discover this weird animal. She studied it, hardly daring to breathe. She noticed how its webbed claws and short legs pushed it strongly through the water. 'Does it come up to breathe?'

'Every few minutes. But it's shy. We'd better move back out of sight,' Mr Hope whispered and waved one arm, telling Mandy to crawl backwards up the bank. But the branch creaked again. This time it cracked and snapped.

'Dad!' Mandy cried. He hung over the creek, his free arm whirling like a windmill, as the bough finally broke.

She saw him begin to topple. He tried to recover his balance, but it was no good. He fell backwards, smack into the water, without uttering a word, a look of complete surprise on his face. The platypus shot off into the shadow of the far bank.

Mandy crawled towards him, her blonde hair falling into her face. She stretched out to catch a hand or foot. 'Grab hold, Dad!'

He surfaced, shook his head like a dog and thrashed about to find his balance. 'It's OK; I can stand up,' he gasped. Water spouted from his mouth.

Mandy began to giggle. Her laughter welled up from deep down, gurgled into her throat and exploded out of her mouth in a great guffaw.

'What was that?' Mandy's mum, Emily Hope,

came flying out of the white house. She ran through the long shadows towards the noise.

'A platypus!' Mr Hope's eager voice hailed her. 'Over here. We just saw our first platypus!' His white T-shirt ballooned out in the water, air bubbles frothed all around.

Emily Hope came to a stop at the top of the bank. She stared down at the scene and turned a puzzled look on Mandy. 'What's your father doing in the water?' She stood, not expecting an answer, hands on hips, her long red hair glowing in the sunset.

'Why not ask him? Hey, what swims like a fish, lays eggs like a reptile, and suckles its young like a mammal?' Mandy quizzed, a grin like a slice of melon splitting her face.

'No, don't tell me, let me guess!' Mrs Hope joined in the joke. 'I'm sure of one thing; you don't mean your dad!'

'Correct.' Mandy finally managed to grab his hand and began to haul him, dripping and spluttering, from the stream. 'Guess again.'

'Let me see, I think you must be talking about a member of the *Ornithorhynchidae* family.' Mrs Hope's own mouth twitched with laughter. 'Found only in Australia. Known as "the living fossil", more often called the duckbilled platypus!' She helped Mandy to pull Adam on to dry land.

'Yes!' Mandy jigged round the acacia tree that had let her father down. 'We saw one. We did. We really saw one!'

'*Ornithor* . . . what?' Mr Hope ignored his dripping clothes, hair and beard. 'Where did you find that out?'

'I looked it up, in the surgery. Come and see.' She slipped an arm round his waist. 'It's safer than looking for it in the wild.'

'But not as much fun!' Mandy got back down on to her hands and knees, then stretched full-length on her belly. She gazed into the water, waiting for the platypus to return.

Her parents went off into their new temporary home; the vets' practice at Mitchell Gap, just outside Eurabbie Bay in New South Wales, Australia.

The house was white, single-storeyed, and built of wood, with a veranda and cool shutters over the windows. There was a swimming-pool out in the 'yard'. Opposite the house, in the shade of the gum trees, was a separate block where the family would work for the next six months. The Hopes were doing a six month exchange; Animal

Ark for Mitchell Gap, Welford for Eurabbie Bay.

The Mitchell Gap surgery was modern and well run, like Animal Ark back home in Welford. The people of Eurabbie Bay brought their pets here, but the Hopes knew that local farmers also brought their animals for treatment. Rob Munroe, the usual vet, had warned them to expect wombats and possums, as well as the more regular sheep and cattle.

'You won't get wombats in Welford,' Adam Hope had told the Munroes.

'But you will get Mrs Ponsonby and her Pekinese,' Emily Hope warned.

'Give me a wombat any day,' Mandy muttered, though in her heart she knew she was going to miss old Pandora and her fussy owner, along with all her other friends back home, especially her best friend, James Hunter.

She would write to James about the platypus, she decided now, as she lay stretched out on the warm red earth. In just a few minutes, when the ripples on the stream had smoothed out and the mud on the bottom had settled. After she'd stayed there long enough for the platypus to come back.

She waited and waited. Dusk fell. And sure enough, the platypus eventually made its lonely way upstream, a dark underwater shadow, nosing in the mud, paddling, twisting and turning in its endless search for food.

> *Kookaburra sits in the old gum tree-ee,*
> *Merry, merry king of the woods he bee-ee . . .*

Adam Hope warbled in the bathroom. He'd showered and was changing his clothes.

Mandy came in, sighing with pleasure. 'I think the platypus has made its burrow near to where Dad fell in.'

Emily Hope, already dressed for the evening in a cool white dress and a long string of turquoise beads, sat in a rocking-chair on the veranda. 'Near the acacia tree?'

'Yes. Will she lay her eggs there?'

'If it *is* a she.'

Their voices murmured on, beneath the rich, pom-pomming voice of a happy Adam Hope.

> *Laugh, kookaburra, laugh, kookaburra,*
> *Gay your life must be!*

Doors creaked and slammed, drawers rattled inside the light wooden house. At last he came out, dressed in a pale blue shirt and dark blue trousers. 'Ready?' He eyed Mandy's dust-covered T-shirt.

'Why, where are we going?'

'Next door. To a barbecue.'

'Next door where?' Mandy looked out across the swimming-pool and the creek, up the tree-lined hill to the far horizon. There wasn't another house in sight.

'To Waratarah, the Simpsons' place,' her father said, putting on an Australian twang. 'It's practically next door, only a few clicks down the road. No worries.'

'A few clicks?' Secretly Mandy longed to stay here at Mitchell Gap. She was hoping for another glimpse of the platypus after supper.

'Kilometres. Clicks. Look lively, mate.'

Her mother gave her a sympathetic look. 'Yes, I know, people aren't half so interesting as animals. But we have to go and meet our neighbours sometime. Better to get it over with.'

So Mandy trudged inside and put on a clean blue and white striped T-shirt. She splashed some water over her face, gave it a quick pat dry and came out again, still wishing she could stay behind.

'Matching family,' her dad said.

'Huh?'

'Blue and white. A matching set.' He jollied her along towards their red Landcruiser parked in the drive. 'Hop in the back. Let's go.'

Soon they were surging and jolting up the rough, corrugated road towards Waratarah. They crossed deep gorges and glimpsed the Pacific Ocean in the distance as they drove the few kilometres north-east of Mitchell Gap.

It was their first barbecue, set in Abbie and Don Simpson's yard, on a hilltop with a breathtaking moonlit view of the sea. Eurabbie Bay lay glittering beneath them, with a wide curve of sandy white beach and a cluster of houselights shimmering between the dense trees.

Guests gathered around Don Simpson's pride and joy – his brand new pool. Don was in the pool-building business, Abbie told Mrs Hope. He also built tennis courts. None of the family was animal-minded.

'Gary's thirteen, about the same age as your Mandy, but he's sports mad. Boogie boarding; that's his thing. Last year it was cricket. Next year, who knows?' Abbie Simpson described how life for the kids in Eurabbie centred on the beach, especially in the school holidays. 'Mandy's lucky.

She's arrived at half-term, just in time to learn boogie boarding for the summer.' She smiled at Mandy and chatted on.

In spite of the amazing view of the ocean with its distant roar, and the soothing smell given off by the gum trees, Mandy lost interest. She wandered off to the quiet side of the pool to listen out for lizards sneaking through the undergrowth, or for the call of a night bird in the dark trees.

'I wouldn't go out there if I was you,' a voice said from behind.

Mandy turned. 'Why not?' The speaker was a boy with curly fair hair, grey eyes and a laid-back stare. He was dressed in long shorts and T-shirt, like all the kids round here.

'Because I found a king brown just down there by that big rock last week. You wouldn't want to go stepping on him now, would you?'

'Wouldn't I?' Mandy admitted her ignorance. 'Why not?'

The boy sighed. 'Poisonous.'

'A snake?'

'That's right. Deadly. The one I found had his stupid head stuck in an empty Coke can. He was rattling around blind, couldn't see a thing.

Couldn't eat, couldn't drink. I reckon he was starving to death.'

'Poor thing.' Mandy sized the boy up. He seemed a bit too casual and blunt for her liking. Personally she thought it wasn't the snake who was stupid, but the person who'd thrown the Coke can away without thinking.

'No worries. I held him tight by his neck and cut him free with a penknife. He went off, no problem. He's most likely still out there under those old eurabbies, waiting for a decent meal to show up.'

She thought again about the boy. After all, her first impression wasn't always right. He did say he'd rescued the snake.

'Gary Simpson,' he told her with a lazy smile. 'You from the vets' place at Mitchell Gap?'

'Yes, I'm Mandy Hope. Do you live here?'

'Sure. You wanna come boogie boarding?' He didn't wait for an answer. 'I'll lend you a board. You have to throw it down on top of a wave and slide on, like this.' He threw himself down on the ground, elbows out, hands clutching an imaginary board. 'You ride the wave, but you gotta watch out for the rips.'

Mandy stared. 'The rips?'

'The undercurrent. It can pull you down, just like that.' He sprang to his feet. 'You wanna come?'

'Yes!' Mandy nodded, unable to resist a challenge.

'You wanna swim?' Gary jerked his thumb towards the empty pool.

'Now?'

He nodded.

'OK,' she agreed. It broke the ice of being new to Eurabbie. Soon all the kids and some of the adults had joined them in the pool. Afterwards, there would be food and drink under the stars, and even Mandy was beginning to think it had been worth giving up the platypus for.

She was having fun swimming underwater in the deep end when she came across another lithe shape. The two of them popped up together, and Katie Browne introduced herself as the practice nurse at Mitchell Gap. 'I live here at Waratarah. I'm a lodger with the Simpsons,' she explained. 'It's handy for work. I can cycle over, no problem.'

Mandy liked Katie staight away. She was young and fit, with short brown hair streaked blonde by the sun. Her eyes were hazel and her face broad and smiling.

'You're lucky, living on the spot at the Gap. You

get to see all the action. Hey, come over here with me.'

They swam to meet a crowd of people gathered at the poolside.

'This is Graham. Graham Masters. He runs the rescue centre at Peppermint Hill. Graham, this is Mandy Hope. She'll help run Mitchell Gap for a few months while the Munroes are away in Yorkshire.' She turned to Mandy. 'You two will bump into each other before long. Graham brings injured animals over to us if he thinks they need to be seen by a vet. Kangaroos, wombats, that sort of thing.'

Mandy smiled up at him. Graham was about thirty, with short brown hair and a wide, white smile. 'We saw kangaroos on the drive up from Sydney,' she told them.

'Yeah,' Graham nodded. 'Roos are pretty friendly guys. You gotta watch out for them on the road.'

'But no wombats.' Mandy was still longing to come face to face with some of Australia's best known animals. 'I don't even know what a wombat looks like.'

'They're fat and furry, a bit like koalas. Slow old things.'

Katie took over from Graham and led Mandy on through the group of party guests. 'The kid over there is Dean Peratinos. He's at school with Gary. And this is Suzi and Marianne; they're Dean's sisters. And that's Alistair King, but you'll get to meet him tomorrow at the Gap. He may look ancient to you, but he still works with us.'

Katie was a bundle of energy as she hauled Mandy out of the pool and introduced her to everyone. Soon they got round the whole crowd and came back to Emily and Adam Hope.

'Mum, this is Katie, our nurse.' Mandy had lost all her shyness. 'She's an expert on snakes.' This was something she'd learned straight away, when she told Katie about Gary's king brown.

'Do you know anything about the duckbilled platypus?' Mr Hope asked, diving in with his question.

'The one that lives in the creek?' Katie nodded hard. 'That old girl is due to lay her eggs any day now!'

Soon they were all talking nineteen to the dozen. By eleven o'clock, when it was time to drive home, Mandy loved everything and everyone in Eurabbie Bay. It was a paradise of unspoilt beaches, wild white surf and friendly people. 'No worries,' they said, and they meant it. The whole pace of life was slow and easy, the weather seemed perfect, and inland there was a whole continent waiting to be discovered.

As Mandy piled into the back of the Landcruiser and the car swayed out of Waratarah, past small farms and apple orchards, along the rough dust road to Mitchell Gap, she thought of all the wild and exotic things that Australia held in store. There would be rosellas and lyre birds, emus, echidnas, and of course the famous koala. She really *must* write to James to tell him all about it.

'Mum, do you think we'll see any koalas?' Mandy asked sleepily. She stared up at the dark umbrella of branches overhead.

'Maybe.' Emily Hope breathed in the night-time scents.

'I hope so. I can't come all the way to Australia and not see one.' Mandy sighed deeply.

That first night, instead of writing her letter, she went to sleep as soon as her head hit the pillow. She dreamed of a mother koala sitting at the end of her bed, fat as a jug, with black button eyes, tufted ears, and a tiny, smiling baby clinging to her back.

Two

'Good morning, Mandy!' Emily Hope appeared at Mandy's bedroom door next morning. She carried a glass of fresh orange juice and a bowl of cornflakes on a tray.

Mandy blinked once, then sat straight up in bed. 'What time is it? Is it dawn?'

'Dawn was hours ago. It's eight o'clock.'

Mandy groaned.

'It's OK; relax. No school for two weeks. It's half-term, remember.'

'It's not that.' She climbed out of bed in her strange new room and went to throw open the shutters. True enough, the sun had risen high over the hill behind the creek. 'I wanted to be up in time to go and look for the platypus.' She sighed.

Emily Hope smiled. 'Never mind. Come and help us to get ready for surgery instead.' She put the breakfast tray on Mandy's bedside table. 'I must admit, I'm feeling a tiny bit nervous about our first day at work.'

Mandy stared. Her mother was the unflappable sort. This wasn't like her.

'What if someone brings in a funnel-web spider or a long-nosed bandicoot? And do you know, there are over three hundred species of lizard in Australia? I only know how to recognise one!'

'Oh, fantastic!' Mandy forgot her disappointment over the platypus. 'Did you say over *three hundred*?' She scrambled into her clothes; the striped blue T-shirt and a pair of white shorts, with white canvas lace-up shoes.

'And one hundred and forty kinds of snake.'

'Brilliant.' She knew Katie Browne would be able to deal with these.

'And over a hundred and ten marsupials.'

'Kangaroo, koala, possum, flying squirrel . . .' Mandy counted those she knew.

'Wallaby, echidna or spiny anteater, wombat . . .' Mrs Hope went on.

'Come on; what are we waiting for?' Mandy gulped down her juice and cereal, ran a brush through her hair, then dashed out on to the veranda. 'Maybe someone will bring in a koala!'

'I doubt it.' Her mother didn't want her to build false hopes. 'People don't keep them as pets. They're fussy eaters. They often die in captivity.'

Mandy nodded. 'Maybe I'll see some at the rescue centre then. Katie said she'd take me to Peppermint Hill as soon as we get time.' By hook or by crook she would add koala to platypus in her letters to James.

Her dad was already busy in the surgery, talking to the old vet they'd met the night before. Alistair King was over sixty and he'd retired from full-time work. But he loved his job and was always ready to lend a hand when needed. When the Munroes decided to go off for six months to work in Welford, Alistair said he would be only too pleased to help their replacements settle in at Mitchell Gap. He was tall and upright, with a wrinkled brown face, a nose hooked like an eagle's, and a shock of white hair swept straight back from his forehead. His brown eyes were sharp and twinkling.

'Put your white coat on, Mandy. We're going to

need you.' Mr Hope nodded towards the waiting-room. There was already a long queue of patients.

Eagerly Mandy did as she was told. She glanced through the door. Perhaps there would be a kookaburra or a cockatoo. She spied a little blue budgerigar in its cage, feathers all puffed up, looking out-of-sorts. But there might be a dingo or a dinky little wallaby. No such luck. She spotted a golden Labrador and a Yorkshire terrier. Even she had to admit that this was slightly disappointing.

Still, they soon got into the swing at Mitchell Gap Veterinary Centre. By mid-morning Mandy had helped her father treat the Labrador for a case of mange, a pregnant Persian cat and a hamster with wet-tail. She'd been out to the residential unit at the back to feed a German shepherd dog, and she'd cleaned out the cages of two kittens. Then her mum took her out on a call to see Hilda Harris's tom-cat, Moses.

Alistair King gave them directions. Hilda's tumbledown farm was just a few 'clicks' upstream from Mitchell Gap. 'Wait till you get past the apple orchards; you'll see Hilda's place tucked away by the creek, no worries,' Alistair assured them. 'She'd normally come down here herself, but her old truck's got a flat tyre. Poor old Moses got himself caught up with a kangaroo, apparently. I reckon it took a lump out of him!'

So Mandy and her mum drove up to treat the cat.

Hilda was as beaten-up as the farm, the truck, and her poor tom. She was thin as a stick, gnarled as her old apple trees. A tiny woman with curly white hair, wearing a faded checked shirt and workmen's trousers several sizes too big, she led the way into her musty barn, sweet with the smell of wrinkled apples in the hayloft. In a dark corner, lying in a box of straw, was the old tom-cat. 'When will you ever learn?' Hilda tutted at him. 'If I told you once, I told you a hundred times, Moses, pick on someone your own size. But no.' She turned to Emily Hope. 'It was a roo, you can bet your life. It knocked him flat with its back legs.'

Swiftly Mandy's mum ran her fingers along Moses's sides. He growled and twitched his tail.

'I found him by the creek, laid out like he was a goner.' Hilda shook her head.

Mandy bit her lip. 'How bad is it?'

'No broken bones,' said Mrs Hope. 'Just badly bruised along the ribs here.' She looked inside the cat's mouth. 'He's been a bit traumatised, poor old fellow. You see, his gums are very pale. That means he's in shock,' she explained to Hilda. 'Look, you can see he's shaking slightly. But we don't need to take him into Mitchell Gap. Cover him up, make sure he has plenty to drink and just keep an eye on him for a day or two. He should be up on his feet by then. He'll be a bit stiff, but none the worse for wear.'

Hilda grunted. 'That's another of your nine lives used up, Moses.'

'How many narrow escapes has he had?' Mandy asked.

'I make this fifteen,' the old lady said with a wink. 'I'm sorry you had the trouble of coming up here to see him.'

'Not at all. I'm glad we did. We're just finding our way around.' Emily Hope smiled. They followed Hilda out into her yard.

'Where to now?' Hilda glanced at the sky with an experienced eye.

'Back to the Gap.'

'Good. You won't want to be far from home this avvo.'

Mandy looked up at the perfect blue haze, in response to the old lady's afternoon forecast. She shrugged.

'There's a buster getting up in the south; you'll see. Best get back as quick as you can.'

They said they would take her advice.

'What's a buster?' Mandy asked as they drove away.

'I don't know. I don't suppose it's anything too serious.' They couldn't imagine the perfect weather breaking, not by the look of the cloudless bay. They saw it as they rose to the crest of a hill and looked down on the distant ocean.

But by the time they got back to Mitchell Gap, a strong wind was blowing. It built up all afternoon, and by three o'clock Gary Simpson had rung to say that the trip to the beach was off. He would have to take Mandy boogie boarding next day. 'It's a buster,' he explained. 'Sorry!'

'No worries,' Mandy said down the phone, before she put it down. But she frowned at her dad. 'This is an awful lot of fuss about a little bit of wind, isn't it? I thought Australians were supposed to be tough, outdoor types.'

Katie Browne had overheard. 'Just you wait,' she said. Outside in the yard a gate rattled and banged. Dust blew up the valley, a hot, reddish cloud of grit. 'No one goes out in a buster,' she warned. She made sure all the windows in the surgery were shut. They waited five or ten minutes as clouds swirled in from the ocean.

And then it rained. It poured down and pelted on to the wooden roof. It splattered into the pool and turned the creek into a sudden torrent of swirling mud. It roared off Eurabbie Bay and up the hill past Waratarah to Mitchell Gap. It thundered and pounded and drenched everything through. Then it stopped, as quickly as it had come. Raindrops pattered from the eurabbie trees; steam began to rise from the hot earth. Everything else was silent and still. Mandy sat through it all in amazement.

'That was a buster,' Katie said calmly. 'We get them once a week or so, right out of the blue.'

Mr Hope was impressed. He looked out of the surgery window and whistled. 'Who's this driving up now?' He'd spotted an old Land-Rover churning up the mud on the track. The rain still sluiced from its roof down the windscreen. The wipers went furiously back and forth.

'That'll be Merv Pyke.' Alistair came up behind. 'Yep. That's Merv with his delivery. Never misses a day.'

'Even in a buster?' Mandy watched as a tall, thin, middle-aged man stepped out of the Land-Rover.

'There isn't a fire or a flood that would stop Merv getting through with the supplies,' Alistair insisted. 'He brings bread, milk, eggs, stuff like that. Merv runs the grocery store in Eurabbie.'

Mr Hope went out into the steaming yard to greet the shopkeeper and order their daily supplies. Mandy followed.

Merv fired the questions back at her dad. 'Would that be wholemeal brown, wheatgerm brown, or multi-grain brown? . . . Would that be sliced or unsliced? . . . Full cream or half cream? . . . Litres or half litres?' At last he got the order shipshape. Meanwhile he was obviously sizing up Mandy and her family. He shot sharp looks at them all. Finally they seemed to pass the Merv Pyke test.

'Nice to meet you folks,' he grunted. He allowed a dog out of the passenger seat to sniff around and say hello. It was a greyhound called Herbie, and the thinnest dog Mandy had ever seen. Thin dog, thin man. But the dog was much friendlier than the owner. Mandy fussed over him while the grown-ups talked.

'Do you reckon you'll like it here at the Gap?' Merv asked, still gruff and unsmiling.

'We love it already,' Mandy's mum said. 'The

sun, the beach and everything.'

Merv grunted again. This was stuff he took for granted. Soon he looked at his watch. 'Can't stand around here all day,' he grumbled, climbing back into his Land-Rover. 'These supplies won't deliver themselves.' He roared the engine and backed out in a cloud of diesel fumes. Then he trundled off down the hill.

'A proper little ray of sunshine,' Mr Hope said.

Mandy smiled. 'The dog's nice.'

'Merv's OK too,' Alistair promised. 'He doesn't smile a lot, but he's a dependable sort of bloke. He practically runs the Bay single-handed. He's on every committee in town. If he likes you, he'll put business your way.'

They grinned and went inside for afternoon surgery.

'So far so good,' Mrs Hope gave Mandy's shoulder a squeeze. She turned to Katie. 'I think we're rather hoping for something more exotic this afternoon!'

Katie checked the appointment book. 'How about Vicki Jackson's cockatoo? Or Mal Stalker's wombat?'

Mandy's face lit up. 'Oh, great!' She couldn't wait to begin again. Soon the cars straggled out of town, up the hill to the Gap, and the waiting-room began to fill.

That afternoon Mandy helped Alistair with the white cockatoo; a noisy, fierce bird the size of a large parrot. It had a magnificent yellow crest which it raised on end like a Mohican.

'Shh, Cocoa!' Vicki warned. The bird squawked and pecked sharply at Mandy's finger. Vicki was a serious, dark haired girl of about eleven. She was worried about Cocoa's long claws. They were beginning to curl under and hurt his feet.

Wrapping the bird in a thick towel to protect himself, Alistair showed her how to trim them, then he checked the cockatoo. 'Cocoa's in pretty good shape,' he said.

The bird whistled in his ear. His buttercup-yellow crest spiked up.

Mandy put both fingers in her ears and laughed.

Cocoa strutted along the edge of the treatment table, scolding the strangers.

'Better give our eardrums a rest and take him back home,' Alistair said with a grin.

They helped put Cocoa into his cage, called Vicki's mum from the waiting-room and watched as the cockatoo told them off too for disturbing his day.

'Next!' Alistair called. He turned to Mandy. 'You're in for a treat. Here comes your first wombat!'

She stood back as Mal Stalker led his pet into the treatment room on the end of a short, strong lead.

The wombat waddled slowly in.

'Meet Harry,' Alistair said, taking the lead.

Harry blinked up at her. He was about sixty centimetres high, with stumpy legs and no tail. He was brownish-black, furry, and very, very fat.

Mandy crouched to his level. 'Hello, Harry.' Fat, and like a badger, only brown, with a stubby nose and tiny black eyes. He nuzzled against her fingers.

The wombat gave a coarse, grunting cough.

'Harry's a rare treat for us,' Alistair told her with a smile. He said that wombats, like kangaroos and koalas, were a protected species. 'You need a licence to keep one as a pet, so we don't see that many here in the surgery.' He turned to the proud owner. 'Let's hoist him up on to the table,' he told Mal, a round-faced boy with short, fair hair. 'What's the problem?'

'His back legs have gone all stiff. He can't seem to walk that well.'

'Hmm. Wombats don't move fast at the best of

times.' Alistair examined Harry's short back legs. 'How old is he?'

'Seventeen. Five years older than me,' the boy said proudly.

'Let's weigh him for a start, shall we?'

Together they put the good-natured, lumbering creature on to the scales.

'Twenty-two kilos,' Mandy declared.

'Overweight.' Alistair stood back and studied him. 'That's his problem. He's carrying too much weight, and he may be developing a touch of arthritis in these joints. What are you feeding him?'

'Grass, roots, the usual stuff.'

'And does he dig up his own roots?'

'No, we feed him.'

Alistair nodded. 'You're spoiling him. Let him loose in the yard, make him forage for his own food. That should help keep his weight down. It'll probably ease those stiff joints as well.' He stroked the wombat's coarse hair. 'Well, what do you think?' he asked Mandy.

'He's gorgeous!' Harry nuzzled up close. 'And friendly!'

'That's his trouble,' Alistair explained. 'In the wild wombats didn't have any natural enemies until man came along. Now the farmers think of them as pests, digging up pastures and destroying fences. The poor old fellow is getting quite rare.'

Thoughtfully Mandy scratched Harry's bald round muzzle. 'As rare as koalas?'

'Not quite. They're both a bit thin on the ground though, like your badgers back home. No one's allowed to go round taking pot-shots at these fellows any more.'

Mandy was glad.

'Not that you can imagine anyone ever wanting to.' The old vet spoke gently as he helped Mal to ease Harry back on to the floor. 'Remember, make him dig for his own food, keep an eye on him.' He saw them both to the door.

Mandy watched Harry's broad backside waddle off. She sighed.

'Happy now?' Katie poked her head into the room.

'Yes.'

'But? Did I just hear a "but" in there?'

'Well . . .' Mandy felt she could confide in Katie. 'This is my second day, and I've already seen kangaroos, and a platypus, and now a wombat.' She listed them on her fingers.

'But no koala?' Katie guessed, remembering the conversation at the Simpsons' barbecue.

Mandy nodded.

'Hmm.' She knitted her brows.

'Hmm what?' Mandy felt a little leap of excitement inside her stomach. It sounded as if Katie had had a good idea.

'Wait here!' She opened her hazel eyes wide, then disappeared. A few minutes later she came back and busied herself along some shelves, sorting out medicines and humming a tune.

This was maddening. 'Well?' Mandy asked. Was she going to see a koala or not?

'I've just seen your mum.'

'And?' She found she could hardly talk. Her heart beat fast. Katie was deliberately teasing her.

'Oh, we had a chat about this and that. Your mum went off for a word with your dad. He said it would be fine.' Katie grinned from ear to ear.

'*What* would be fine?' She thought she would burst.

'For you and your mum to take a few days off at the end of this week.'

'To do what?'

'To come with me.'

'Where? Where are we going?'

Katie turned at last and laughed out loud. 'How would you like to come on a bushwalk?'

'And see some koalas? Oh!' Mandy jumped in the air. 'Oh, great! Oh, fantastic! When?' She was dizzy with excitement as Katie told her the details.

That night she did write to James. She told him about the roo bars on all the cars to protect them from kangaroos that shot across the roads without warning. She told him about their mysterious platypus, who had failed to show up that evening, and about the overweight wombat. She finished off her letter by saying that she felt she was the luckiest person alive.

Our nurse, Katie Browne, has invited Mum and me on holiday. We're going on a bushwalk! Up into the mountains, to the Wirritoomba Falls. We're going to camp by the Warraburra River, on the edge of the Blue Peak Wildlife Sanctuary. Katie says we're bound to see some koalas there, though they're quite rare.

James, I can hardly believe it. I'm going on a bushwalk to see some koalas! Isn't that fantastic? I'll write and tell you all about it when I get back.

Lots of love, Mandy

Three

Boogie boarding was fun. But it wasn't as exciting as the idea of going on a bushwalk.

Mandy learned to ride the huge waves lying flat on her belly, choosing the right moment to join the swell and crash off the mighty breakers. All around her, the water rose, roared and broke. Surf foamed, the board dipped, steadied and sped towards the shore.

'Pretty good.' Gary stood on the beach, his board tucked under his arm. 'For a first shot.'

She was glad to be accepted into the gang; Dean and his sister, Suzi, a boy called Sam, and Julie, who was junior boogie boarding champion of

Eurabbie Bay. The days sped by, a mixture of hard work at the Gap and hard play on the beach. Before she knew it, the time for the bushwalk had come.

'Boots?' Emily Hope ticked things off on a list. They were due to set off early next morning.

'Yup.' She lined them up by her bed.

'Thick socks, shorts, two T-shirts, one swimming costume, one waterproof jacket, one sweater.'

'Yup.'

'Undies.'

'Yup.'

'Survival kit, sticking-plaster, insect repellent, water purifiers, sunblock, penknife, string, safety-pins.'

'Yup, yup, yup.'

'Backpack?'

Mandy hauled it from under her bed. She'd been organised and ready to go for ages, packing and unpacking her rucksack to make sure everything would fit in.

'Well done! Let's get an early night then. We have to be up at the crack of dawn.' Her mum kissed her goodnight. 'Katie says she'll meet us in Eurabbie in time for the first bus that heads inland.'

It had all been carefully planned, from the early start on the long-distance bus, out through the farmland that fringed the coast of New South Wales, up into the Warragerri Mountains. Once inland, they would rely on their own two feet, following the Warraburra River and camping for the first night by the gigantic Wirritoomba Falls.

That night, though, Mandy found it hard to sleep. She tossed and turned, got out of bed to check her kit for the fourth time, tried to doze off again. The darkness of the night seemed to last for ever, and she thought morning would never come.

But it did, and then it was a quick breakfast in the half-light, a fond farewell to her dad, who looked for a moment as if he wished he was coming too, and one last check of everything they needed for the four-day trip.

Mr Hope ran them into town. The bus already stood waiting at the stop, with Katie inside. Before long the driver climbed in and they waved goodbye to her father and the Bay.

By the time the sun was fully up, they were rolling through the groves of macadamia nuts, between fields of maize and vines, already leaving behind the last signs of civilisation.

Once past the tiny town of Mitchell, with its one main street, its petrol station, pub and white wooden church, the houses stopped altogether. After that, it was endless stretches of forest, broken only by bright blue lakes, and in the distance the hazy mountains. The bus churned along the rough road close to the river, taking hairpin bends in its stride. Mandy sat with her face glued to the window, spotting a kookaburra, then a whole flock of pretty birds which Katie said were rosellas. They rose from the yellow acacia tree and flew overhead.

'Hear that?' Katie asked.

There was a screaming cry, like a mad laugh, high in the gum trees.

'That's a kookaburra. You can tell why we call him the laughing jackass.'

Mandy didn't admit that the noise had scared her. She concentrated again on looking out for dingoes and kangaroos as the bus crossed a flat plain with open bush and scrub.

It grew hot. She was glad when they left the plain and began to climb into the mountains, into the shade of the huge mountain ashes and the eurabbie trees. At last they reached their bus stop.

'This is it.' Katie stood and swung her backpack from the luggage rack.

Emily Hope and Mandy followed her down the aisle and off the bus. They turned to wave at the driver and stepped out on to the oldest continent on earth.

The Warragerri Mountains were volcanic rocks. Their jagged spires reached high into the dense blue sky. They were thirteen million years old. Katie told them all this as they shouldered their backpacks and set off on foot for the nearby river-bank. Between the rocks were deep gorges and forests where they would make their bushwalk.

Mandy's mum walked slowly and happily behind as Katie answered all Mandy's questions. She ran her hand along the smooth, pinkish bark of a gum tree and stepped off the path to gaze up at the overhead network of leaves and vines. 'I can smell mint!' she called.

Katie stopped and turned. 'That's a peppermint-gum; that's why.'

Mandy went on ahead until she reached the river. She bent to dip her fingers in the cool, greeny-blue water. There, at eye level, she came face to face with her first possum.

It was sleeping in its nest but awoke at the sound of Mandy's approach. She saw the twitch of its ringed, bushy tail in the undergrowth, then its enormous dark eyes and batlike ears. It was the size of a small cat, and to her astonishment she saw that the creature had several babies clinging to her back. The possum stared at her.

Soon Mandy felt Katie creep up from behind to see what she'd found.

'Possum!' Katie confirmed.

They watched together as the creature took a small leap on to a low branch and clung there with its back feet curled like human hands. The four babies, small and ratlike, clung on.

'I think she's spotted something,' Katie whispered.

And sure enough they saw a hawk hovering overhead. It rode the air currents, sweeping this way and that. It spotted its prey; the tasty mother possum and her offspring, and waited for the moment to drop through the air and pounce.

Mandy stood up and waved her arms. There was a rustling and crackling in the undergrowth as several small animals, including the possum, shot off in alarm. In the sky, the hawk wheeled and flew away.

'Phew!' Mandy heaved a sigh of relief. She thought about the defenceless mother.

'You missed something special there,' Katie told her. 'If that hawk had gone for her, she would have played dead. It's called playing possum, you know, for that reason. She goes limp, hoping that the hawk will lose interest. It often works.'

Mandy was intrigued. Still, she was glad that she hadn't waited to see if the play-dead trick would work.

'Let's go,' Katie said. She stood up straight and looked around. 'We follow the river up to the Falls. It's about twenty clicks. We should just about make it by sundown.'

Twenty clicks sounded like an awful lot of walking to Mandy, and it was uphill every step of the way. They set off sturdily, tramping up the rock-strewn path, glimpsing purple, pink and blue orchids, and feeling the heat of the afternoon sun even through the thick canopy of leaves. Mandy's backpack began to rub her shoulders. Thank heavens she'd chucked out a couple of extra T-shirts, she thought. She wondered how Katie managed to stride out like she did. She had their tent strapped to her rucksack, yet she covered the ground like a mountain goat, hardly ever stopping to rest.

By teatime Mandy's legs were aching and the red cotton scarf she'd tied around her neck was soaked with sweat. But she could add echidna to the list of animals she'd spotted. 'It looks like a porcupine,' she told her mum. She ran to catch them up after she'd stopped to watch it digging for insects at the base of a gum tree. 'Or a hedgehog, only with longer spines.'

Ahead they could hear the faint roar of the Wirritoomba Falls.

'How far now?' Mandy gasped. The shadows were lengthening. Her legs began to wobble with the effort of walking uphill.

'Just a couple of clicks,' Katie promised. 'We can freshen up when we get there, no worries.'

They tramped on, hot and weary, longing to reach the Falls. All around, the forest was alive with bats and bandicoots, king browns and flying squirrels. A goanna lizard darted across their path, and a scruffy, ungainly bird came up to greet them. The emu was obviously too curious for its own good. 'Shoo!' Katie whooshed it away, as some larger, unseen animal crept through the nearby bushes. 'Probably a dingo,' she said. The emu ran awkwardly ahead, its long neck dipping and swaying as it went.

At last the waterfall came into view, about ten metres wide, falling from ledge to ledge down forty metres of rock. The cascades were crystal clear against the black layers, dropping into a cool, moist gorge between banks of brilliant green ferns. As the water plunged over the highest cliff, it sent out spray that Mandy felt in the air as they drew near. Soon they stood at the foot of the Wirritoomba Falls, staring up at its great height.

But not for long. Mandy was the first to unlace her boots and kick them to one side. She was out of her clothes and into her swimming costume in a flash. She joined the dozen weary bushwalkers in the clear pool at the base of the Falls, and took a well deserved swim.

This is heaven, she told herself. She swam and ducked underwater, feeling her body slice through the cold clear water. She got out and dived in again from the nearest rocks. She scrambled to a ledge on the Falls and stood under a pure mountain torrent. Then she jumped clean into the deep pool, plummeted down and came up beside her mum, her face tingling, her fair hair fanning out across the surface of the pool.

Then they got out and dried themselves, got dressed and made camp alongside the other tents on a small river-flat downstream from the waterfall. Katie unzipped their tent from its bag and they unrolled it. When they'd threaded the supple rods through their casings, the tent took shape. It looked like a neat canvas igloo, anchored to the ground with guy ropes and hooks that sank easily into the soft earth.

This was their mobile home; bright green, with an arched door-flap and a small window. Inside, there was just enough space for three sleeping-bags. Their cooking pans and stove must stay outside with their rucksacks.

'OK?' Katie stood back and surveyed their sleeping arrangements. She looked sturdy and capable in her boots and shorts.

'Personally, I could fall asleep standing up!' Emily Hope laughed.

'But first let's eat!' declared Mandy.

They took packets of dried soup and cooked them with water fresh from the river. Mandy sipped gingerly at first, then gulped it down. It was delicious. For pudding they had an apple and a chocolate bar.

'For energy,' her mum said.

'You'll need it.' Katie went to wash the pots in the stream. By the time she returned, Mandy had snuggled deep into her sleeping-bag and was staring up at the green dome of their tent. It wasn't long before Katie and her mum crawled in too.

'Cosy?' Emily Hope asked. Mandy nodded. The three of them lay quietly as the light drained away and night fell.

'What happens tomorrow?' Mandy asked drowsily.

'We head for Blue Peak and the wildlife sanctuary.' Katie yawned. 'I'll show you on the map in the morning.'

Mandy nodded. 'Isn't it quiet?'

Katie lifted her head. 'Shh. Your mum's already asleep.'

They fell back into a dark silence. But then a

sound broke into their riverside paradise. It was loud, harsh and grating, like a saw cutting through wood.

'What's that?' Mandy sat bolt upright. She hoped that Katie would answer, that she was still awake.

'Nothing. Go to sleep, there's a good kid.' The reply was sleepy and muffled.

She lay quiet. 'There it is again!' It sounded like some kind of strange animal, but none that she'd ever heard before.

The cry grated and sawed through the air. 'Awwgh . . . awwgh . . . awwgh!

'Katie!' Mandy whispered. She felt her skin begin to prickle with goosebumps.

'For Pete's sake, Mandy, I'm trying to get some sleep!' Reluctantly she leaned up on her elbows and began to listen.

'There!'

'Awwgh . . . awwgh!'

'Oh yes, that,' Katie said sleepily. 'I know what that is. That's a koolewong, the one you're so keen to see. A bangaroo, a little old colo. That's what it is.' She lay down to sleep once more.

'You mean a koala?' Mandy strained to hear it again. Out there, somewhere in the gum trees, was her dream come true. A koala bear gave out its weird, grating cry, perched under the stars, many metres above the bush. 'Awwgh . . . awwgh!' Snuggling its baby on its back, clutching a branch, it was calling out a promise.

There were koalas very near, timid and gentle, but waiting for her to come and see them. 'Tomorrow,' she promised herself, curling up to sleep, drifting off to the sound of the wild water and the weird cry.

Four

Next day Mandy was up bright and early. The moment she crawled out of the tent she began searching the treetops, wandering up and down the riverbank, looking in vain for any sign of the noisy koalas.

'No luck?' Emily Hope joined her. She handed Mandy a mug of hot tea.

'No, but I heard them. I know they're there!' This morning she was hopeful. She smiled at her mum, who looked relaxed and happy, her hair done up in a rough ponytail, a towel slung round her neck.

'I'll have a quick splash, then we'll break camp

and get an early start.' Mrs Hope went with her towel and toothbrush to the water's edge.

Mandy took one more look at the tall gum trees; no, the koalas must have curled up in the high branches well out of sight, all set to sleep away the long, hot day. Mandy sighed and went to help Katie to dismantle the tent.

By eight o'clock they were on their way. Katie had shown them their route on the map, across country through a narrow gorge to Blue Peak Wildlife Sanctuary. It was a walk of about fifteen kilometres. 'Not all uphill today,' she promised. 'And boy, is there a treat in store for you when we get there!' She folded the map, tucked her sun-bleached hair behind her ears and they began the day's march.

On this second day of their bushwalk Mandy took everything in her stride. She forged ahead along leafy tracks, spotting lizards and echidna galore, feeling the trees and bushes buzz and flutter with life. Occasionally Katie would join her to point out the way, or to show her some strange rock formation, while Emily Hope pottered along behind.

'How far now?' Mandy asked, impatient to arrive. She gazed across a long slope where fingers of rock cast deep shadows, and waterfalls showed up like thin silver ribbons against the rich green trees.

'Half an hour. See that tall rock shaped like the blade of a knife? That marks the southern boundary of Blue Peak. The flat plain beyond is all national park.'

Mandy nodded. 'Come on, then!' They should be there by lunch-time. She showered more questions on poor Katie. 'Who runs the nature reserve? What kind of animals will we see? How long will we stay there?'

Katie reined her back. 'Whoa! Just wait and see. I'll take you along to meet Mike Macdonald. He's the chief ranger at Blue Peak. With a bit of luck he'll be free to take us out in his Land-cruiser.'

At last they reached the sharp rock, next to a narrow road where a sign read 'Blue Peak Wildlife Sanctuary. All Visitors Report to the Ranger. Watch Out for Kangaroos!'

Emily Hope nodded thankfully. 'We're finally here!'

Together they walked across a flat area of grass and scrub. Mandy and her mum followed Katie to a low wooden office building where they were introduced to a short, stocky man with crinkly brown hair and a firm handshake.

'Hi, Mike. This is Emily and Mandy Hope. They're over from England. I've promised Mandy her first sight of the old narnagoon.' Katie winked. 'Koala, that is.'

The strange Aboriginal name sent a tingle down Mandy's spine. She smiled at a girl of about her own age who had come out of the office on to the veranda to see what was going on.

'Good, good. I reckon we might just manage that.' Mike slipped his hands into the pockets of his denim shorts and nodded at the girl. 'My girl, Cherry here, knows all the best spots for koalas. Why don't we all hop in the motor and cruise around for a bit?' He glanced up at the high sun. 'Mind you, they don't like the heat. What's that old saying about mad dogs and Englishmen?' He grinned and helped them up one at a time into the open-topped four-wheel drive vehicle.

'Hi.' Cherry smiled shyly and sat down next to Mandy. She was as slight and petite as her dad was stocky and strong. Her dark, short, curly hair framed her face. Her eyes were wide and grey, her face covered in light freckles.

'Hi.' Mandy hung on as they drove off. She was too excited to say much.

'My gran lives in Perth, Scotland,' Cherry told her. 'I went there two years ago.' She spoke softly, beginning to point out to Mandy the herds of kangaroo that grazed in the open spaces. She called them 'mobs'.

Mandy asked about the gangs of yellowy-brown, skinny wild dogs that roamed through the bush.

'Dingoes,' Cherry confirmed.

One threw back its head and howled at their approach.

Mandy noticed the dingoes' pointed ears, the brown, intelligent eyes and sharp muzzles. They were roughly the size of collie dogs back home, with loose, rangy limbs and long tails. 'Are they very fierce?' she asked.

'Not against us. They don't exactly like humans, but they won't attack us. You don't want to believe everything you hear,' Cherry said. They watched as a pair of the wild dogs loped out of sight.

'Which way now?' Mike glanced over his shoulder.

'Take the track up to the left, towards the ridge with the spotted-gums.'

They held tight as Mike turned the Landcruiser

and they lurched off-road up a narrow, rocky path.

'There's a whole bunch of them feeding on the spotted-gums,' Cherry explained. 'That's all they eat, so I always know where to find them.'

Mandy puzzled over this. 'You mean, they won't eat peppermint-gum leaves, or eurabbies?'

Cherry shook her head. 'No. Only spotted-gums. They know what they like!' She smiled. 'The funny thing is, they all smell exactly the same close to!'

'What do they smell of?'

'Cough sweets! It's the eucalyptus. Spotted-gums, eurabbies, peppermint-gums; they're all different kinds of eucalyptus.'

'It's true!' Katie laughed. 'Hey, I think we made it!'

Mike stopped and wrenched on the handbrake. They all jumped out. They were in a tiny clearing, surrounded by spotted-gums. Here there was plenty of food and shade for the koala colony. But Mandy was disappointed to find at first that, true to their shy natures, they had chosen not to come down to greet them.

'Just you wait,' Katie said with a wink.

They sat on a felled tree-trunk, dappled by the sun, patiently and quietly waiting.

After five minutes a face did peer down at them from a high branch. 'There!' Cherry whispered.

Mandy held her breath. 'Will it come down?'

'Maybe.'

They were in luck. The koala swung itself on to the trunk and descended feet-first. It clung with all four feet, and to Mandy's delight it carried a baby with it. As the koala reached the ground, she seemed to glance at them, then began to lick the earth slowly and thoughtfully.

'Why is she doing that?' Mandy whispered.

'We think it helps her to digest her food,' Katie explained. 'No one knows for sure.'

'Come on!' Cherry encouraged Mandy to move closer. There were more koalas coming lazily to the ground, even approaching their group to find out what treat lay in store.

'They're really tame!' Mandy whispered.

'That's because they're used to us round here,' Cherry said. 'They trust us.' She walked confidently towards the mother koala and stooped to stroke the baby. The adult turned and stretched out her arms to be picked up, snuggling just like a teddy bear. She seemed to sigh in Cherry's arms. 'Take the baby,' she whispered. 'But watch out for his claws!'

Gently Mandy lifted the warm little creature from its mother's back. The fully-grown koala was quite big, about sixty centimetres high, but the baby was still only half that size, with softer brown fur and the sweetest smiling face. He peered at Mandy from between his chubby cheeks and tufted ears. 'Oh!' She was speechless. The baby clung to her, perfectly content.

'See, they do smell of cough drops!' Katie came up with her own adopted koala. 'Well, what do you think?'

Mandy simply shook her head. She studied her koala's dark, bear-like snout and tiny, shiny eyes. She felt the strength of his grip around her shoulder. Gently she went on stroking it. 'See how sharp his claws are,' she whispered to her mum.

'I expect it's for gripping the tree-trunks. Look, I think yours is falling asleep!'

Mandy nestled her cheek against the koala's soft, furry head. Sure enough, he was settling into her arms, ready for a good long rest.

Mike came to join them. He said he thought the baby was about a year old and nearly ready to leave his mother. Cherry showed them the mother's pouch. 'It faces downwards,' she explained. 'Not upwards, like in a kangaroo.'

'You'd better give him back,' Mike said. 'Mum looks ready for a nap herself.'

Cherry put the mother down and Mandy handed the baby over to her. He swung himself up, piggy-back style, blinked once at Mandy and let himself be carried off across the clearing. They watched as the mother took a lazy look at the eighteen-metre spotted-gum, reached out, and with a grip like a vice clawed her way slowly up. She climbed in a series of jumps, about a metre and a half at a time, until at last she reached the first fork in the trunk and settled in for her lunch-time nap.

Afterwards, Mandy felt that she needed a couple of minutes to take in what she'd just seen. She wandered away a short distance, shaking her head, smiling to herself. Now, wherever she looked she could see koalas curled in branches, fast asleep or peering lazily down. When she returned to the group, she found Katie making plans to take Cherry bushwalking with them, on a yomp round the boundaries of the nature reserve.

'That is if you'd like to come,' she said kindly.

Cherry smiled. She checked with her dad and accepted. 'I can show you more koala colonies,' she told Mandy. 'We can camp overnight at Glen

Ives, just outside the park. They go diamond fossicking there.'

'Hang on a moment.' Mrs Hope interrupted the flow of enthusiasm and strange words from the two native Australians. 'What's this "yomping" business?'

'It's a kind of fast walk. A cross between a walk and a run actually.' Katie made it sound easy.

Emily Hope groaned. 'It sounds like torture!'

They laughed. 'You'll love it!' Katie got out the map to study the route. 'Here's Glen Ives, just here.'

'And what's this "diamond fossicking"?' Mandy was curious too. She saw from the map that the tiny town was by a river in what looked like pretty steep countryside.

'It's looking for diamonds on the bed of a stream,' Cherry told her. 'We can have a go if you want.'

'Diamonds? Real diamonds?' Mandy asked. 'Are they worth loads of money? Does anyone ever find any?'

'Sometimes,' Cherry shrugged. 'Not very often. It's a good laugh though.'

So with this to look forward to, they parted from Mike Macdonald. Cherry looked likely to make a good guide as they continued on the second day of their bushwalk.

Fossicking was fun, as Cherry had said.

'Better than yomping?' Mandy asked her mum.

Mrs Hope groaned. '*Anything*'s better than yomping, including being boiled in oil, I expect. But Katie likes to see me suffer, that's all.' She was cooling her aching feet in the fast-running stream after their rapid march across rough country. Meanwhile, Cherry and Mandy turned over rocks and picked through pebbles, their wrists and hands numb with cold.

Every now and then, someone up or downstream would let out a small squeal of surprise, followed soon after by a disappointed grunt. The rough, shiny little stone carefully separated out from all the dull brown pebbles turned out not to be a diamond after all. The precious gems were few and far between. But bushwalkers were a hopeful lot and sometimes spent hours after a day's walk through the Blue Peak Wildlife Sanctuary up here at Glen Ives, fully expecting to make their fortunes.

Glen Ives itself was outside the boundary of the nature reserve; a small mining town and a meeting place for folks from the coast whose hobbies included fossicking and playing country music.

When the sun went down, Mandy and her group headed for the only bar in town. Katie ordered 'stubbies' for herself and Emily Hope. Mandy saw with interest that these were small cans of cold beer. The girls had Fanta straight from the fridge. A bunch of Queenslanders down from the north set up a singsong. They made the English visitors join in the only song from the outback they'd ever heard. It was about a jolly swagman sitting by his billabong. Mandy laughed and smiled her way through it, enjoying the friendly gathering and the homespun guitar music.

Then, when her eyes would hardly stay open a moment longer, she heard Katie fall into conversation with one of the men. Their nurse joked along as usual, then her face suddenly turned serious.

'That can't be right,' she said with a frown.

'It's right enough, mate.' The man sniffed and rubbed his chin with his thumb and forefinger. 'That's the way I heard it!' He was about Katie's age, an easy-going type with a baseball cap and a surfing T-shirt.

'Did you hear that?' Katie leaned across to Mandy, Cherry and Emily. 'Robbie reckons they're gonna set up a big mining company here. The full works, not just bits of fossicking here and there. They're gonna turn the place into a proper mining operation.'

'Meaning what?' Mrs Hope asked the Queenslanders.

'Meaning a new road down from the north, cutting round the edge of Blue Peak, straight up the mountain into the town. It's going to come whack through the middle of the forest.' Robbie told them all he knew.

Mandy turned to Cherry. 'Did you know about this?'

She nodded. 'They finally got permission to go ahead last month. Dad's cut up pretty rough about it, actually.'

'But they won't bring the road through Blue Peak?'

'No way. We're protected by the government. Like Robbie said, they'll have to cut in from the north.'

'And they can actually do this?' Mandy's mum sounded annoyed. 'Start up an industry on the edge of a national park?'

'And an animal sanctuary?' Mandy thought it would be a disaster.

'As long as they steer clear of the boundary.' Katie looked glum. 'The worst thing is, they'll have to cut down some trees.'

'Well,' said one of Robbie's friends. He tried to cheer them up. 'You got plenty of trees round here. I reckon you can afford to lose a few, no worries!'

But they were still upset by the news. Soon afterwards, they said goodbye to the crowd in the bar and headed back to camp. A light breeze rustled overhead, and twice they heard the loud cry of a koala.

They got back to base, a silent crew. They sat in a quiet huddle beside the tent, gazing up at the stars.

'You see,' Katie explained, 'I reckon myself that they'll have to cut down some pretty special trees on that far side of the valley. I don't know for sure, but aren't there spotted-gum and jarrah on that slope?' She turned to Cherry with a questioning look.

'That's right.'

There was another long pause. Suddenly it clicked. Mandy could see why Cherry and Katie were so down in the dumps. '*How* special are those trees?' she gasped.

'Well, the spotted-gums aren't such a big problem.' Cherry had obviously given this a lot of thought. 'We've got plenty of spotted-gums in the reserve. You saw them. It means we can easily move those Glen Ives koalas to Blue Peak.' She hesitated.

'But?' Mandy guessed what was coming next. She answered for her. 'But if there are koalas living off the jarrah trees in Glen Ives, are you saying that you don't have any of that type of tree to move them to?' She knew now how vital it was for each group of koalas to be moved to their own special type of gum tree.

Cherry nodded sadly. Her grey eyes began to fill with tears.

'And are you sure they won't eat anything else?' Mandy appealed to Katie, who shook her head.

'And *is* there a colony of koalas living in the Glen Ives jarrahs?' Mrs Hope tried to keep some common sense in the discussion. A fear had spread through their small group.

'I reckon so.' Cherry's voice had faded to a whisper.

'But if the mining company cuts down their

trees to build a road, that means they'll have nothing to eat!' Mandy cried.

Her voice echoed through the dark clearing, but met no reply. The rare and timid creatures, so loving and trusting, were prisoners of their own fussy diet. They would only eat jarrah leaves, and now the diamond miners would move in to destroy their habitat. The jarrah koalas would starve to death!

Five

The first thing they had to do was to make certain that Cherry's fears were true. If there *were* koalas living in the jarrah trees at the back of the tiny mining village, they needed to know how many were actually in danger.

'No one knows for sure,' Cherry said. 'Dad and the other rangers have been out to check *all* the gum trees, but it's hard to get it right. He thought he saw koalas in the jarrahs. But, there again, he had his mind fixed on counting the ones he already knew about in the spotted-gums, the mountain ashes and the peppermints. They've got a big job on their hands, trying to move so many.'

She whispered to Mandy in the half-light before dawn the next day. Emily Hope and Katie still slept soundly.

As the minutes ticked by and the sky grew lighter, Mandy thought hard. 'Now would be the best time to go and find out, wouldn't it?' she asked. 'Before the sun comes up. That's when the koalas are easiest to find.'

'Yes.'

'Do you know the way?'

'I reckon so.'

'And can you recognise the jarrahs?'

'Reckon so,' Cherry said again in her low, soft voice. 'Some surveyors came up to Glen Ives the other day. They left stakes in the ground all the way up the mountain. That's the track for the new road.'

Mandy was already half out of her sleeping-bag and pulling on her T-shirt and shorts. The idea of counting the koalas was the first step towards saving them. No way was she going to let this road ruin their lives, not if she could help it. She'd spent most of the night promising herself that she wouldn't let it happen. 'How far away is it?'

'Not far. A couple of clicks at the most.' Cherry scrambled out of her own sleeping-bag. Together they got dressed and crept out of the tent into a quiet world wet with dew.

'Hang on, I'll leave a note.' Quickly Mandy unzipped the front of her backpack. She delved into it for a pencil and notepad, then scrawled a message for her mum and Katie, telling them where they had gone. 'Back in about an hour,' she wrote. They left the note pinned to the tent flap with a safety-pin from Mandy's survival kit. 'OK, let's go!' she whispered.

She followed Cherry on to a track which led to the town. The whole place was deserted, almost ghostly in the morning mist that clung to the steep ground. The two girls ran across the narrow road, by the side of the church and on to another narrow track towards the tumbling stream, where only yesterday fossicking for diamonds had seemed such harmless fun. A kookaburra clattered from a low branch, its wings beating and clacking like a wooden rattle in the still dawn. Mandy jumped.

Cherry turned to wait. 'You never know, we might hit lucky,' she whispered. The stillness all around made them anxious to keep their voices down.

'How come?' Mandy was breathless and on edge.

'Maybe my dad got it wrong. Maybe he never saw koalas in the old jarrahs.'

Mandy sighed. She thought Cherry was kidding herself, trying not to believe the worst. But she didn't say anything. For a while they jogged down the steep slope in silence. 'You know something?' she said, as Cherry stopped to get her bearings. 'I've got my fingers crossed. I never thought I'd say this, but today for the first time I'm hoping that we *don't* find any koalas!'

Cherry nodded. Her small, pointed face was deadly serious. 'Me too. This way; we're nearly there.' She cut away from the stream, beating down ferns with a long stick and striding through the tall grass.

'We'll make it just before the sun comes up.' Mandy could see that the tips of the far mountains of the Warragerri Mountains were tinged with a golden-red.

'There!' Cherry pointed to a line of tall wooden stakes loosely joined by a thick orange and white plastic tape, running down the slope into the valley bottom. 'That gives us a pretty good idea of where the road will be.'

'Now, where are the jarrahs?' Mandy didn't know enough about the eucalyptus trees to tell one type from another. She felt confused and edgy, glad that Cherry was there to lead the way.

They ran deep into the forest, following the line of bright tape. In the dawn, the cough-sweet smell of the leaves was stronger than ever. Mandy had a sense of eyes watching them from every direction, and sure enough, as they slowed down for Cherry to identify the trees she caught sight of a lonely koala ambling from one tree-trunk to another, chewing thoughtfully as it went. Then there was another and another, a small colony of them, some with small babies, and one large boss male who gathered his harem about him as the two girls approached.

They watched with bated breath to see which trees the koalas would choose to climb.

'Spotted-gum!' Cherry breathed, as slowly the short, stout legs grasped at smooth trunks, and sharp claws dug into the bark. 'No worries, we can rescue these!'

Mandy nodded and breathed again. A few more metres down the slope they came to some unusually tall, straight trees. Cherry slapped the palm of her hand against the nearest one and peered up into the wide umbrella of branches.

'Jarrahs?'

She nodded. 'I can't see any koalas up there, thank heavens!'

Quickly they went from one jarrah to the next, about a dozen in all, scanning the branches, praying *not* to see any of the cuddly grey shapes peering down at them with their black button eyes.

'What's so special about the jarrahs?' Mandy wished she understood why koalas were such fussy eaters, and why there weren't many of this type of tree around. It made the task of helping koalas to survive so much more difficult.

'I don't exactly know. You find them up in Queensland mostly. It's a hard, jungle type of wood.'

They searched on, beginning to believe that these rare trees weren't home to any families of koalas. It would mean they could relax. They would trust Cherry's dad and his rangers to move the other koalas safely to trees in the Blue Peak reserve.

But then Mandy caught hold of Cherry's arm. 'Wait!'

A slow old koala shuffled down the hill towards them. He stopped to lick the earth, then caught a handful of tender young shoots growing from the base of a tree. He spotted the girls and waddled

towards them, ears twitching. Cherry put out a hand to scratch his head. His eyes closed and he sighed.

'Hello, old boy,' Cherry whispered. She took the bunch of leaves from his fist and looked up at the tree. 'It's a jarrah,' she told Mandy, her voice flat.

Mandy's heart missed a beat. Soon a couple of agile young koalas appeared from the topmost branches of the same tree and began to descend. One was a mother with a tiny, hairless baby peeping out of the pouch.

'One, two, three.' Slowly Mandy counted. 'Four, including the baby.'

'Five, six.' Cherry pointed. Not far away, another female sat astride a branch, back legs dangling, while a larger baby tried out its claws by hanging upside-down from the same branch.

In the end they counted ten koalas. Cherry reckoned there were two males, five females, and as far as they could tell, three babies, from the tiny, hairless one to the cheeky youngster already almost weaned. They watched him greedily tuck into the predigested food his patient mother delivered into his open mouth. This was the halfway house between the baby feeding on mother's milk and being fully weaned.

'Ten.' Mandy sadly repeated the total. 'At least!' They'd spent the best part of an hour searching and counting. Now all of the koalas had climbed out of sight into the jarrahs, and the forest was coming alive with other sights and sounds. Radiant blue butterflies rose with the sun and fluttered from flower to flower. Lizards darted on to flat rocks to sit and bask. 'What shall we do?' Mandy asked. She felt that her worst fears had come true.

'I guess we'd better get back and tell the others.' Cherry dug the toe of her boot into the soft ground. Disappointment made it hard to speak.

'And then back to Blue Peak to tell your dad!'

Mandy realised they needed help. 'Listen, Cherry; now that we know for sure that they're up there, don't you think he'll know of somewhere they can go?'

'Maybe.' She shrugged. 'I reckon he'll try his best.'

Cheered by this thought, they said goodbye to the koalas and trudged back up the slope, through the village to their campsite, where they found the kettle coming to the boil, and Katie and Emily Hope bent over the map, busily discussing their day's route.

The news about the jarrah-tree koalas changed all their plans, however. Katie saw straight away that they must put off their bushwalk and concentrate on getting something done about the endangered animals.

'Why can't they change the route of the road?' Mandy asked, angry that so-called progress should be put before the safety of wildlife in the area. 'After all, the koalas were here first!'

'No need to remind me,' her mum said. 'I'm on your side. I think it's mad. But that's the way it goes. It's too late now to get up a campaign to stop the road; the government's already made up its mind.'

'And it's nothing new,' Katie reminded them.

As Mandy listened, she got rid of some of her anger by beating air-pockets out of the canvas and rolling up their tent.

'Once there used to be millions of the little fellows. Now it's down to thousands.'

'What happened?' Mrs Hope slid tent hooks into a specially made bag.

'Disease. And man. That's what happened to them. We have a lot to answer for.'

Mandy looked up. 'Did people hunt them?'

Katie nodded. 'For their skins. And then there were the forest fires and the land clearances. Everything's been against the poor old things!'

'All the more reason for us to save this little group!' Mandy argued. She got to her feet with a determined glint in her eye. Her old fighting spirit had revived. 'If the koalas need jarrah trees, then jarrah trees is what they'll have.'

Katie smiled. 'Good on you, kid.'

Soon they were packed and ready to start off along the same track that they'd travelled the day before. They made good progress in the cool of the early morning. Well before lunch-time, the blade-shaped rock at the entrance to the Blue Peak Wildlife Sanctuary appeared in the distance. The four of them put on another spurt, anxious to share their news with Mike Macdonald.

When they reached the reserve, Cherry and Mandy ran across the yard, ahead of Emily Hope and Katie. A different ranger, a young, sandy-haired woman, sat with Mike, taking a break in the shade.

'Don't tell me you struck it rich!' Mike stood in the doorway, hands on hips, grinning broadly. 'Is that why you hightailed it back here so soon?'

'No!' Cherry gasped out the story of the jarrah-tree koalas. 'Honest, Dad, we're dead sure. There's ten of them up in those trees. Mandy and I went out there early this morning. We counted them!'

The young woman looked up sharply. Then she stood and went inside. Mike's face fell. 'You sure?' he asked. 'Cast-iron, copper-bottomed certain?'

They both nodded urgently. 'Maybe we could get the builders to put off starting work on the road until we find some more jarrah trees?' Mandy pleaded.

Mike gave Emily Hope and Katie a worried glance. He shook his head. 'No way. They've planned this road building down to the last dollar. Monday is their starting day, and Monday it's got to be!'

'But that's only three days from now!' Mandy's voice shook with alarm.

'That's right. Three days for Miriam and me to get as many koalas safely over to Blue Peak as we can. I reckon there's more than fifty in those eurabbies and peppermint-gums. We'll have our work cut out, but we reckon we can do it. We got five this morning. We'll be back at sundown, aiming to bring in half a dozen more.'

He explained to Mandy that there was a lot of red-tape and paperwork involved. For the last few days he'd been busy identifying just how much wildlife was under threat from the road. Besides the koalas, there were four species of snake, more than twenty flying squirrels, and many wombats dug into the hillside. Now that they'd finished counting, and Miriam had filled out the dozens of necessary forms, the evacuation could begin.

'Are you saying there's no time to find homes for the jarrah-tree koalas?' Emily Hope asked.

'We'll try. That's all I can promise.' He scratched his head and turned to Cherry and Mandy. 'You two did a good job identifying this latest colony, but you've given us an extra headache, I have to admit. For all I know, the nearest jarrahs could be thousands of kilometres from here, way up in

Queensland. And to tell you the truth, we just don't have the time to start looking.'

'You could always evacuate them along with the rest and then try them on some other food,' Katie suggested. 'I read about koalas eating mistletoe once!'

Mike's smile was brief. 'When it comes down to it, I reckon that's what we'll have to do.'

Mandy realised that he didn't sound too hopeful. In fact, it sounded as if he was so busy with other tasks that he was ready to admit defeat on her koalas. It seemed as if they were just one problem too many.

'Hey, Mike, why not let me ring round some of the other reserves?' Miriam suggested from inside the office. 'I can get on the phone to Fort Worth and Murrigo, to see what they reckon.'

'Good idea.' Mike looked as if anything was worth a try.

'Katie?' Mandy sidled up to ask another vital question. 'You know those koalas you mentioned who were fed on mistletoe?'

'Hmm.' She stood, feet planted wide on the dusty ground, hands on hips, waiting for Miriam to come back. They all hoped it would be good news.

'How long did they live on their new diet?'

'Not long,' she admitted. 'I won't lie to you, kid. If we don't find jarrah trees for these fellows, their chances are pretty slim.'

Again Mandy's heart sank. She felt her mum come up behind her.

'They're doing their best,' Mrs Hope whispered. 'Let's just hope we're in luck.'

They all stared eagerly at Miriam as she came back on to the veranda. She shook her head and shrugged. 'They say the same as us; they don't know of a single jarrah tree between here and Queensland.'

'And nothing to the west?' Katie asked.

'Only mountains and desert,' Mike said glumly.

They stared at one another, feeling helpless.

Miriam sighed and leaned against the doorpost. 'Sorry,' she said. 'I guess it's pretty tough news.'

'But we can't just do nothing,' Mandy decided. She realised that the rangers cared about the jarrah koalas, but they had to solve the easier problems first. But she and her group still had a choice. They could turn away from the koalas at Glen Ives and carry on their bushwalk holiday as planned. They would see all the wonders of the forest, then meet up with the bus in time to take them home on Sunday evening. It would be back to work at Mitchell Gap on Monday as if nothing was wrong.

But there was another way forward, and it flashed into Mandy's mind as the thing they must do. They could cut short their break and head straight back to the Gap. They could pick up the Landcruiser there and rush back west to the mountains. And they could spend the whole weekend combing the area, up every track, across every acre of scrubland searching for the elusive jarrah trees. Just four or five would be enough. They could evacuate the koalas to their new homes and know for sure that they would live contentedly in the topmost branches, swinging and climbing, chewing their precious jarrah leaves. Half a dozen special trees to save the lives of ten koalas! That was all they needed.

She turned to her mum, full of eager determination, and began to explain her plan.

Six

Mandy told them her idea, then she held her breath. Would the others agree to give up their holiday to save her koalas?

Mrs Hope listened. She didn't break in or cut Mandy short. She turned to Katie.

Katie's eyes narrowed. No one said a word. Then the nurse gave a sharp nod. 'Got you! Great idea!' She put up both thumbs and gave an enormous grin.

'Hey, what's going on?' Mike's voice rumbled across the yard. He came up and put an arm round his daughter's shoulder.

Cherry gave a small grin. 'I reckon you'd better ask Mandy.'

She came straight out with it. 'We're planning to find new jarrahs for the Glen Ives koalas!' Her eyes sparkled, she felt clear and confident.

'Just like that?' He glanced sideways at her mum. 'Dead easy!'

Emily Hope smiled. 'There's one thing about Mandy,' she told him. 'When there are animals in trouble, you can bet your life she'll be in there fighting to save them.'

Meanwhile, Mandy went to talk to Cherry. 'How would you like to come on the jarrah search with us?' There must be huge areas of unexplored forest on the slopes of the Warragerri Mountains. Surely somewhere, in some unvisited gorge, up a wild mountainside, they would find what they were looking for. 'We need you,' she urged. 'You're the one who knows most about the area. Will you help?'

Cherry seemed to grow a few centimetres taller. Back went her shoulders. Up went her head. 'You just try and stop me!' she said.

'You know something, I think Mandy's finally met her match,' Mrs Hope told Katie. 'Cherry's as crazy about animals as my own darling daughter, and the two of them have set their hearts on this.'

'Then I reckon we can't fail!'

Katie's chirpy reply gave their confidence an extra boost. Even Mike's doubts seemed to vanish. He offered them a lift from Blue Peak to the bus route. 'What time does the bus to Eurabbie come along on a Friday?' he called to Miriam, who was still inside the office.

'Midday.'

Mike glanced at his watch. 'We'll make it, no worries.' He left the patient Miriam with the task of finding some uninhabited spotted-gums inside the sanctuary for their five rescued koalas, then they all jumped in the Landcruiser and headed off for Wirritoomba.

The road took them the long way round, through scrubland and skirting round the steepest hills. But well before midday they arrived by the banks of the Warraburra River. Mike dropped them at their bus stop and wished them luck.

'Good on you,' he told them. 'We're run off our feet trying to get things done before the bulldozers move in. We need you lot to look out for those koalas.' He nodded, gave Cherry a hug, climbed back into the car and roared off back to Blue Peak.

They sat by the roadside, staring up the winding track for a sign of the Eurabbie bus. Behind them, the river tumbled and gurgled over polished boulders; a temptation for them all in the midday heat. But Mandy stuck it out. She gazed along the shimmering road, scarcely able to sit still and wait in her eagerness to be off on the next leg of their journey. Katie went off towards the riverbank and came back with an armful of ferns.

'Use these as sunshades,' she advised.

They took them and found they came in useful as fans and flyswats too. The minutes ticked by.

'I hope we didn't miss that bus,' Cherry said. There was hardly any traffic on the road. A wagon went by with a trailer full of logs. A farmer drove his tractor out of a side turning.

'No; here it comes!' Katie squinted into the far distance. There was a flash of light as the sun caught a windscreen, and they heard the far-off chug and grind of the diesel engine. At last, the almost empty bus appeared.

Katie, Emily, Cherry and Mandy scrambled on board with their backpacks. The driver recognised them. 'G'day! I reckon you all had to turn back because you got blisters!' he joked.

Katie pulled Mandy down the aisle before she could explain their mission. 'No time for that,' she warned. 'We gotta get a move on here.'

They flopped down into seats close to the front. The driver was in a chatty mood. He wanted to know about England and their cricket team. He was cricket mad.

Mandy felt herself lulled into a daze by the swaying bus. She heard dimly the driver telling her mum that there was a buster brewing up later that day. He pointed eastward. 'See that cloud?'

Emily Hope screwed up her eyes and admitted she couldn't. 'It looks clear blue to me.'

'No, there's a speck of cloud there, see. That's a buster. It's gonna hit us before we get into Eurabbie.'

Katie raised her eyebrows. 'The man's right,' she agreed. 'Just our luck.'

The bus swayed and lurched towards the coast. By three o'clock even Emily Hope had to admit the clouds were gathering. They rolled across the sky from the east, the colour of a purple bruise. A wind buffeted them. The first fat drops of rain fell.

In seconds they were caught in a downpour. The windscreen wipers whirred and swished. Gallons of water seemed to fall in seconds.

'It's like being in a car wash!' Mandy said. There was something thrilling, even a bit frightening,

about the force of the rain.

But the driver had to signal to pull up. He couldn't see the road ahead. Rain gusted and splattered against them. They must sit it out and wait for it to pass.

The delay set them on edge. Precious time was being lost. They needed to get back to Mitchell Gap, explain their mission to Mr Hope and Alistair, and be on the road in the Landcruiser again before nightfall.

For half an hour they sat and endured the storm. Then it cleared, as quickly as it came. The driver started the engine.

'How far is it to Eurabbie now?' Mandy asked him.

'Fifty or sixty clicks. Less than an hour away.' The storm didn't seem to have put him out in the least. They lurched back on to the road, he cleared the screen and they continued on their way.

Mandy frowned at Cherry. 'Can't this old thing go any faster?' she grumbled.

'Shh!' Cherry warned. She turned bright pink.

'Steady on.' Mrs Hope turned and smiled. She knew there was nothing they could do. 'When we get into town, I'll give your father a ring to tell him what's happened.'

'How can you bear to be so patient?' Mandy cried.

'Because!' She settled into her seat for the final stretch. 'Because there's not a thing we can do about a buster.'

When they arrived in Eurabbie late on Friday afternoon, and Emily Hope rang home, there was no reply. 'Your father must be out on a call,' she said, swinging open the door of the telephone booth. 'What now?'

'Hang on a couple of ticks!' Katie stepped from the kerb and began to flag down passing motorists. Soon a van splashed to a halt in the huge roadside puddle. 'Yes!' Katie grinned triumphantly. 'I thought it was! It's Merv Pyke. Hi, Merv!' She greeted him brightly. 'You going up Mitchell way by any chance?'

He seemed to scowl as he leaned over and wound down the window. 'How's that?'

'I said, any chance of a lift up to Mitchell Gap?' Katie jerked her thumb at the group of them. 'It's kind of urgent, Merv.'

He nodded briskly. 'In the back,' he ordered. 'Good job I've nearly finished my deliveries.'

So they all crowded in beside the half empty racks of bread and cartons of eggs. Katie sat up front with Merv and Herbie. 'The smell of that bread's making me starving hungry!' she confessed.

'A pity I haven't loaded up any spare loaves,' he growled. 'Otherwise I could've sold you one.' The van began the long climb out past Waratarah towards the Gap.

'Merv, I don't suppose you could help us?' Katie went on, undeterred. 'I was wondering; have you ever heard of any jarrah trees growing this side of the Queensland border?'

'Strike a light!' he tutted. 'I've heard some mad

things in my time, but that just about beats the lot!' He shoved the van into second gear.

'Does that mean you haven't?' Mandy leaned forward.

He shook his head. 'That's right, I haven't. And if there *was* a jarrah tree in Eurabbie Bay, I'd know about it!'

'That's right, he would.' Katie turned and nodded. 'That's why I asked.'

Mandy's hopes began to fade. It seemed as if her plan wasn't so promising after all.

'Try inland,' he suggested.

'The Warragerris?'

'Yeah. There isn't a cat in hell's chance of finding one this far east. The mountains might be different; I wouldn't know.'

At last they drew into the yard at the veterinary centre. Merv handed Mrs Hope their order of bread, milk and eggs. She paid him and he set off on his way.

'Thanks for the lift,' Katie called.

'Jarrah trees!' he muttered, shaking his head. Herbie yapped at them from the passenger seat. They all gave a wave, relieved to spy the tall, red shape of Mr Hope's Landcruiser come through the gates as Merv left.

Mandy's dad parked and climbed out. 'What brings you back so early? Not that I'm not delighted to see you!' he added. He herded them inside the house, said hello to Cherry and caught a few of Mandy's garbled words. 'What's this about koalas?' He turned to Emily Hope. 'Jarrahs? Bulldozers? Do I gather that Mandy's got a rescue mission underway?'

'Yes, but before you go off like a firework, Mandy, why not take Cherry out for a quick swim in the pool to freshen up? Leave me and Katie to fix things up with your dad. Go on. And we'll eat a proper meal before we do anything else, OK!' She shooed the girls off to Mandy's bedroom to change into their swimming gear.

They cooled down in the pool and had a rest, while Adam Hope prepared a fresh salad, with cheese and Merv's fresh bread. They ate outdoors on the veranda, overlooking the pool, catching up on home news.

Her dad and Alistair had run the surgery like clockwork, he assured them. Hilda Harris had rung in to report that Moses, her tom-cat, was up and about after his scrap with the kangaroo. There was a letter from James waiting for Mandy on the kitchen table. She ran to fetch it, and read that all was well in Welford. James was taking his dog, Blackie, on long country walks. He said that the Munroes had arrived at Animal Ark and settled in well. Mandy had a pang of homesickness, then tuned back in to her dad's conversation.

'And guess what? Alistair tells me that the platypus had already laid her eggs, a few weeks back. She's been scurrying in and out of her burrow near the acacia tree. It looks to me like she's getting ready to bring her babies out into the stream.' He said he'd spent a happy evening watching the busy mother come and go.

Mandy shot to her feet once more. 'I've finished, thank you very much. That was lovely!' She brushed crumbs from her T-shirt and fidgeted from foot to foot.

Adam Hope laughed. 'Why don't you take Cherry along to see if you can find the platypus?'

'Great!' No sooner said than done. They scrambled off together, and soon had their noses pinned to the roots of the old acacia tree. In no time at all they'd spotted the narrow entrance to the burrow. They crouched there patiently, waiting for the platypus to emerge.

But Mandy found she was torn between longing to see the strange, blunt bill appear at the hole, and wanting to get back to the Warragerri Mountains. 'You could come back and see her another day,' she suggested after ten minutes or so.

Cherry nodded. 'I'd like that.'

As if drawn by a magnet, they returned to the veranda. They found that while they'd been by the stream, their neighbours, the Simpsons, had called in for a chat. Abbie Simpson sat with a glass of wine. The two men had opened cans of beer. Gary sat with his feet dangling in the pool, relaxed as ever. 'G'day!' he greeted them. 'Wanna come boogie boarding?'

'We can't.' Mandy sat down beside him. 'Gary, this is Cherry Macdonald from the Blue Peak Wildlife Sanctuary. We only came back to pick up the Landcruiser. We have to drive back to the mountains tonight to save some koalas.' She tried to sound matter of fact, but her eagerness came through.

Gary looked at her as if she was mad. 'How do you reckon on doing that?'

She told him.

'And these jarrah koalas, they're just gonna walk into your arms all nice and cuddly, and come along with you to their new homes, are they?'

Mandy admitted that she hadn't thought that far ahead. 'First we have to find the trees.'

'And you reckon they're worth all this trouble?' He was amazed that they'd cut short their bushwalk for a bunch of koalas.

Mandy splashed water at him with her foot. 'You wouldn't say that if it was ten *people* we were trying to rescue, would you?'

'No. But koalas aren't the same as people.'

'To me and Cherry they are. In fact, there are loads fewer koalas in the world than people. That makes them even more important!' She sounded quite definite.

'It takes all sorts,' he muttered, splashing her back.

'Watch it!' Cherry yelled, caught in the crossfire.

'I'd like to see *you* giving up a weekend to help someone,' Mandy challenged. 'But I expect you're too busy boogie boarding.'

'I reckon I am,' Gary agreed happily.

'Even if I said we needed as much help as we can get?' Mandy had an idea that Gary was more interested in the koalas than he let on. She remembered how he'd risked danger to free the king brown snake from the drink can.

'How come?'

'Well, we could split up and cover a bigger area if there were more of us,' she pointed out.

'But it's miles away from the beach in those mountains. No surf. Nothing!'

'There are waterfalls.' She gave him a long stare.

'OK, so I guess the waves will still be there when I get back.' He shrugged and began to look thoughtful. 'But Dean and Suzi said to meet them at the beach in the morning. . . . Still, I reckon they could go ahead without me . . . You say these koalas will starve to death when their trees are ripped up?'

Mandy nodded hard.

'And you know what a jarrah looks like?' He turned to Cherry, his forehead over his grey eyes wrinkled into a frown.

'Yeah.'

'And it's definite; they won't eat anything else?'

'Nope.'

'Hmm.' He stood up. 'I reckon I might just come along.' He shoved his hands into his pockets and strolled across the yard to arrange things with his parents.

'Good on you!' Cherry grinned at Mandy. 'I never reckoned he would.'

Mandy looked wise. 'I did. He's got a secret soft spot for animals!'

And so they sorted Gary out with a tiny one-man tent and a sleeping-bag. By early evening they'd filled up the Landcruiser with fuel and were ready to wave goodbye to Mitchell Gap. Alistair had rolled up with his own battered four-wheel drive for use at the surgery. The two men were sure they could survive the weekend without help.

'Good luck!' Mr Hope stood on the veranda to watch them set off. Mandy's mum was driving, Katie sat alongside, and the three kids piled in the back with the camping gear. 'And take care!'

Mandy turned to watch him as they pulled out of the yard. She waved. Finally they vanished round a bend in the road. Then she looked ahead. They had a good few hours' driving in front of them, in the half-light and then in the dark. They'd already had a long and tiring day. But she felt good sitting alongside her two new friends. Cherry and Gary had joined up with her to do something really important. They would pull together and try their very best.

'This is it!' she whispered. She glimpsed the clear outline of the rugged mountains and felt her chest tighten with excitement as the car sped past farms and orchards. 'This is really it!'

The search was on.

Seven

They drove west into the setting sun. Katie and Mrs Hope shared the driving along the familiar road. 'We'll drive until we drop,' Katie said. 'Then we'll make camp overnight and set off again before dawn tomorrow.'

Mandy guessed they'd be lucky to get five or six hours' sleep. They sang as they drove, and played 'I spy' to keep alert.

'I spy with my little eye something beginning with "k"!' Emily Hope set them off.

'Kangaroo!' came the immediate chorus. Mandy got in first and she took over. 'I spy with my little eye something beginning with "b.k."!'

'Bare knees!' Katie guessed.

'No.'

'Blonde Katie?' Cherry had a try. The others wrinkled their brows.

'No. Do you give in?'

'Yes,' they said at last.

'Baby kangaroo!' Mandy crowed. She pointed to the bush. All around herds of kangaroos wandered and grazed as the sun went down. They cast long shadows over the reddish brown earth, and every so often a young kangaroo would pop its head out of its mother's pouch, then retreat into warm safety once more. 'See, they're everywhere!'

Gary gave a little snort. ' "B.k." Baby kangaroo! It should be "j.", not "b.k." '

'Why?' Mandy gazed at the tame herds. Some kangaroos were grey, but some had a reddish tinge, and some were even blackish-brown. They seemed to be constantly eating or looking for fresh grass, leaves, bark; anything they could sink their teeth into. When they spotted a likely bush they would leap towards it on their powerful hind legs, using their tails to balance. Then they would tear at the leaves with their forepaws and chew, chew and chew.

'We don't say baby kangaroo, we say joey,' Gary explained patiently.

'OK then, you have a turn,' Mandy suggested.

He came up with, 'Something beginning with "k"!'

They groaned. 'We've had that already,' Cherry said.

'Nope.' He shook his head. 'This isn't the same.'

'Keys!' Emily Hope pointed to the ignition switch.

'Nope.'

'Knuckles,' Katie said.

'Nope.'

'Inside the car or out?' Mandy needed a clue.

'Out.'

'Kookaburra!' She was struck by the bird's laughing call above the sharp, barking cough of wombats, the cry of dingoes.

'Yep!'

'Where?' Cherry demanded. 'I can't see one!'

'OK, then, 'I hear with my little ear . . . !'

The game fell flat. Tiredness crept over them. 'Want me to take over?' Katie volunteered for a spell of driving. It was nine-thirty, pitch dark, and the air was still noisy with strange, piercing calls. Creatures rustled through the undergrowth as she hopped down to change seats with Mandy's mum.

She drove for a quarter of an hour or so, a pop-music station playing quietly in the background. Mandy was leaning sideways out of the open window, staring up at the stars in the black sky. The wind whipped her hair from her face. She felt fully awake. Suddenly she saw a rush and blur of movement up ahead. A small herd of kangaroos was cutting across the bush, towards the road, coming at full-speed. They came in great leaps and bounds. 'Kangaroos!' she yelled.

They rushed at the car from Katie's blind-spot. She hadn't even seen them.

'Stop!' Mandy warned. 'Katie, stop, quick!'

The big kangaroo at the head of the bunch seemed hypnotised by their headlights. He leaped out of the scrub, straight into their path.

Katie slammed on the brakes. The tyres squealed and crunched over the loose, unmade surface. They swerved to the left, sliding off the road into the bush.

'Hang on in the back!' Mrs Hope shouted.

They grabbed the roll-bars and felt the car continue on its swerve. Then there was a jolt and shudder as the engine cut out. Tilted at a crazy sideways angle, headlights glaring across the scrub, the driver's-side wheels spun and whirred.

'Did we hit anything?' Katie cried, her voice faint and shaken.

'No. You missed.' Mandy scrambled to the back window for a view of the retreating herd. 'They're all OK!' She watched them race off into the darkness, raising a cloud of dust as they went; twenty or thirty animals loping off at high speed.

'Is everyone all right?' Emily Hope checked.

They all said they were fine, unhurt by the mad lurch into a gulley, two wheels stuck in the air.

'How do we get back on to the road?' Cherry asked.

'All get on to my side of the car for a start,' Katie said, recovering her nerve after the shock of the near miss. 'We need as much weight as we can, to rock ourselves upright!'

They shifted to one side, pulling tents and backpacks with them. Mrs Hope clambered out of the passenger seat to join them. With her extra weight, the Landcruiser sank back into its proper position, all four wheels on the ground. Then Katie restarted the engine, checked the lights for damage, put the car into gear and drove slowly forward over the rocky surface. She edged out of the gulley on to the raised road. 'Back on firm ground!' She heaved a sigh of relief.

'Look at that!' Gary laughed out loud. He pointed to a roadside sign caught in the glare of their headlights. 'Watch Out For Kangaroos' it said, in bold red letters.

The others joined in the laughter. 'You can say that again!' Mrs Hope breathed out. They all praised Mandy for keeping her eyes peeled. Mandy felt pleased with herself, but embarrassed by the attention. She felt herself blush under cover of darkness.

'What do you say we make camp for the night?' Katie suggested. 'We don't want to push our luck.'

They all agreed to look out for a flat, safe area. They drove slowly on, their lights the only ones to pierce the intense blackness of the bush at night. At last they came to a side track leading to a small lake fed by a stream from the foothills of the Warragerri Mountains. The fresh running water made it an ideal place to stop.

Soon they'd parked up, unloaded their gear and pitched their tents. By eleven o'clock they had crawled into their sleeping-bags, exhausted by the day, nervous about the task that still lay ahead.

'Sleep well,' Mandy's mum murmured as she zipped the tent and snuggled down for the night.

But the others were already fast asleep, lulled by the shallow waves which lapped the lake shore.

They were up before dawn as planned, splashing themselves awake in the cold, fresh water, gulping down hot tea and bread. They were on the road by five, in the grey and misty light, the long road to the mountains winding ahead. This morning no one felt like chatting or playing games to pass the time. It was already Saturday. On Monday the bulldozers moved into Glen Ives.

Their aim was to spend the day searching as much territory as they could cover, hoping to find the vital jarrah trees. Cherry reminded them exactly what they were looking for. They were to ignore the patchy, scaly bark of the spotted-gums, and to concentrate on anything tall, straight and smooth. 'The leaves are flat and kind of spear-shaped. They're glossy and tough-looking.'

'Like laurel leaves back home,' Emily Hope suggested.

Prepared as well as they ever would be, they approached the foothills. Katie navigated them off the beaten track, reasoning that if they were to stand a chance of finding the rare trees, it would be in an area which no one had explored. 'Off the

bushwalking tracks, somewhere deep in the forest.'
They decided to head for Mount Warragerri itself;
the highest mountain in the range. They would
drive as far up its tree-covered slopes as possible.
After that they would use the car as a kind of base
camp, and go off in separate directions, returning
to check in every two hours or so.

'I reckon I should go off solo to the east.' Katie
scanned the landscape and took charge of the foot
expeditions. She'd parked the Landcruiser in a
small clearing, at the edge of a long drop down a
sheer cliff of volcanic rock. All around, trees
formed a thick canopy, their tall trunks stretching
for the light. 'And you four should split into pairs
and go off, up there, and there.' She pointed to
two more possible tracks. Though rough and
unused, they could see where animals had worn
down the soft earth and pushed a way through
the undergrowth. 'Use your compasses, and
remember to check in.' She looked at her watch.
'The first time we meet up here will be at nine
o'clock. Has everyone got that?'

Mandy felt glad to trust Katie's judgment of the
territory. It was lucky that their nurse was such a
keen bushwalker.

They split up, Katie to the east, Emily Hope

and Cherry to the west, and Gary and Mandy heading north up the slope, zig-zagging and using their height to gaze out across the treetops. Sometimes Gary led the way. He stepped out confidently and tackled steep slopes without a downward glance. Sometimes Mandy would suggest a swing to the west or east if she saw an area of different coloured leaves which was worth investigating. Once they caught sight of her mum and Cherry in a clearing way below. They raised their arms and yelled.

'No luck?' Emily Hope called.

'Not yet. How about you?' Mandy cupped her hands around her mouth to shout back.

'No! Keep looking!'

An hour passed without success; an hour and a half. Soon it would be time to return to base. Mandy felt a small stab of doubt. She gazed up. They were surrounded by gum trees. They spread for hundreds of kilometres to the west, high into the mountains, way beyond the Great Dividing Range. But not a single one seemed to be of any use to the Glen Ives koalas.

What if they searched all day without any luck? What if there were no more jarrah trees to be found? What then?

She sighed. Then a tiny movement caught her eye. She was distracted from her task. 'Look at that!' she breathed.

Gary crept to her side. 'What?'

'Up there, look! There's something staring down at us with great big eyes. It's got a bushy tail like a squirrel. Can you see?'

'Yep, sugar glider,' he said, matter-of-fact.

It ran daintily down the tree-trunk from its high branch, then picked at the bark for grubs. It was silvery-grey with a dark stripe down its back, and its splendid tail was as long as the whole of the rest of its body. Mandy thought it was beautiful, with its pointed ears and upturned nose, its forefeet grasping its meal like human hands. 'Is that the same as a flying squirrel?'

He nodded, less caught up in gazing at their shy visitor. The glider looked, and caught sight of them again. It twitched its tail in annoyance. 'Looks like we interrupted her breakfast.'

And then the sugar glider did the most amazing thing. It rested itself back on to its haunches and launched itself into mid-air!

Mandy gasped and staggered a couple of steps backwards into a clump of ferns. She stumbled against a hidden rock. Overhead, the glider spread its legs wide and opened up a parachute of skin between its front and back limbs. It was flying, or rather floating from one tree-trunk to another, covering an incredible distance. Its white underside looked for all the world like a giant underwater stingray as it glided a hundred metres and landed, gripping the new tree with its sharp claws.

'Wow!' Mandy sat down hard on the rock. 'Did you see that?' She marvelled at the unpowered flight.

Gary turned to look at her. He tensed up. 'Mandy, don't move!'

Something told her to obey.

'Don't put your feet down. Keep still!'

Mandy peered down between her knees to where Gary was pointing. She stayed still as a statue. There was a slithering movement through the ferns, a glimpse of shiny brown. Then she saw a snake raise itself from the ground, its flat blunt head turned in her direction, about a metre from her left foot. 'What is it?' she whispered.

'Shh! Don't move! King brown!' Gary himself stood rooted to the spot. 'I'd know it anywhere. Looks like you tripped against his rock, worse luck.'

'Will he bite?' She stared into the snake's eyes. His tongue shot between his thin lips and flicked towards her. Her legs began to ache from holding them in one position.

'I don't reckon he's too pleased.' Gary tried to ease the tension. But sweat had begun to stand out on his forehead. 'How much longer can you stay there?' he whispered.

'I'm OK,' she insisted. She dare not break her gaze. Every flick of the snake's tongue, every arch and squirm of his spine could mean danger. She didn't move, yet her muscles ached, her mouth was dry, her hands clutched the rock and the sweat began to trickle down her back.

She sensed that Gary had begun to back off, out of range of the king brown's striking distance. She swivelled her eyes after him, breaking away from the snake's gaze. She saw him seize a sturdy stick from the ground. It forked into two sections. He broke these back to a length of three or four centimetres each. He worked swiftly. 'Quickly, Gary!' she pleaded softly. The snake was still reared up at her, poised ready.

With the forked stick in his hand he crept forward. When he came within range he raised it like a spear. 'I'll say jump and you jump! Roll backwards off that rock quick as you can!' he ordered. 'I'm going to try and pin his head down, but you'd better make a pretty fast move, just in case I miss!'

She nodded. *Please don't let him miss!* she prayed. Her life was in his hands.

'Ready?' He glanced up at her from his crouching position.

Again she nodded.

'Jump!' he yelled. He sprang forward and stabbed at the snake with the pronged stick. He trapped the head on the ground. The snake slithered and writhed under the stick. Mandy rolled backwards, hit the earth, kept on rolling. Then she sprang to her feet.

'Gary!' she called out in a sudden fresh panic. He was out of sight on the far side of the rock. Everything fell silent.

Then she saw him leap at the lowest branch of the tree that the sugar glider had launched herself from. He caught it and swung himself up to safety. He straddled the branch and gave her a thumbs-up signal. 'It's OK, no worries!' he called, keeping a wary eye on the escape route of the king brown.

'Has he gone?'

He nodded. 'He's headed straight for that crack

in the big rock over there.' He pointed to a sharp boulder some distance away. 'I reckon we're safe enough now.'

Mandy's legs felt shaky as she walked to meet up with Gary at a safe distance from the boulder. 'Thanks,' she said. She was breathing hard, feeling drained.

'You glad I decided to come along?' he asked cheekily.

'You bet!' She didn't bother to deny it, she was just too relieved. This was her second near miss in less than twenty-four hours.

'That was a bit of a tight spot,' he confessed. 'What do you say we get back to base now and check in with the others?'

She nodded. 'Maybe someone will have some good news.' She tried to look on the bright side.

'I wouldn't bet on it,' Gary said, striding off, one hand in his pocket, whistling as he went.

'Well, we've still got all day.' She caught up with him, careful to stick to open ground, away from the sinister shadows of the rocks.

'Yup,' he nodded. He gave her a grin. 'No worries.'

Mandy relaxed. This 'no worries' outlook was catching. Soon they would all meet up at the

Landcruiser, study the map, try again. The whole day lay ahead. Out there some jarrah trees stood waiting. She just had to have faith and keep on looking. She grinned back at him as they loped together down the slope.

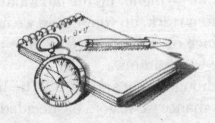

Eight

Katie was the last to check in at their Landcruiser base. It was ten-past nine. She came trekking towards them, her stride still full of energy and determination. 'I've spotted every blessed tree on this planet except a jarrah tree!' she reported. 'I saw some mountain ashes over twenty-five metres high, I reckon. And acacias as far as I could see!' She shrugged.

'What now?' Mandy refused to feel down. She'd kept quiet about her narrow escape from the king brown; there was no point in worrying her mum. 'Which way shall we try next?'

Katie shaded her eyes with her hand and

scanned the tree-covered slopes. 'Let's think this through. If we go higher up the mountain, further off the beaten track, do you reckon we have more or less chance of finding jarrahs?' She turned to Cherry for her opinion.

Cherry thought long and hard. 'The higher we go, the less chance we've got,' she decided. 'Jarrahs grow where it's hot and wet, remember.'

Mrs Hope nodded. 'Good point. They grow in the jungle up in Queensland.'

'Right,' Katie agreed. She got out her compass and stared thoughtfully at the dial.

'If they like the heat, maybe we should keep to the lower slopes,' Mandy suggested. 'And if they like the wet, let's head for the rainiest spots.'

'That would be the eastern side of the mountains,' Katie said. 'The busters come in off the Pacific Ocean, remember. And they blow themselves out here in the Warragerri Mountains. The eastern slopes get all the rain.'

'That's it then. We head east.' Mrs Hope climbed into the Landcruiser and waited for the others to join her. 'Let's drive in the direction of that narrow gorge. I think I can see a stream coming off the mountain into the valley. It should be nice and wet down there.'

They set off, clinging to the sturdy roll-bars as the car covered the rough ground, lurching into gullies and climbing out again, wheels spinning, engine whining. The sun was already hot. The Landcruiser broke through virgin forest. Bright flashes of red and green flew squawking from the low branches of eurabbies and peppermint-gums. Two flying squirrels leaped and floated under the green canopy of leaves.

'Wow! Look at that!' For a moment Emily Hope was distracted. She stared after the sugar gliders.

'Mum, watch out!' Mandy warned. She spotted an echidna bumbling along in front of them. He heard the car, felt the ground tremble beneath his feet and stopped dead in his tracks. Up went his long spines in self-defence.

Her mum slammed on the brakes. They skidded to a halt, churning up dirt as they slewed sideways. The front wheels were only a metre away from the prickly echidna. The engine cut out as they waited for him to get out of their way. Gradually his spines relaxed, he snouted in the loose earth for ants, then toddled out of sight.

'Close!' Cherry breathed, her eyes wide.

'This whole place is alive with animals!' Mandy marvelled. White cockatoos with yellow crests called down at them as they passed by.

A few minutes later, Gary pointed out a proud lyre-bird strutting through the bush, his tail feathers on display. 'They're pretty rare as a matter of fact,' he explained. 'I reckon it's a good sign.'

'How come?' Mandy craned sideways to watch tho bird's courtship dance.

'You generally come across them in the rainforest.'

'Like the jarrah trees?'

He nodded.

'Don't you think it smells damp around here? Or is that wishful thinking?' she asked. They'd dipped down into the gorge, into the shadows. Creepers clung to the tree trunks, and broad flat-leaved vines hung from the boughs. The air had a heavy, muggy feel, sweet with perfume from the bright pink blossom.

'It does! It definitely smells and feels damp!' Katie confirmed. 'Let's drive down and check out the stream. Keep your eyes peeled, everyone!' She studied the map as Mrs Hope drove the last leg. 'This is the stream, here, to the north-east of Mount Warragerri. It's called the Wallacha.'

'And it's gorgeous!' Mrs Hope pulled on the brake.

They sat for a moment, feeling the humid heat. They watched the clear water tumble from rock to rock. Here the trees grew so close together that they sat in semi-darkness, surrounded by tree-ferns and palms, beneath the soaring gum trees.

Then once more Katie sent them off in pairs, up the sides of the gorge. They tramped, climbed, searched and returned two hours later. Still no luck. They drove up the far side of the gorge into the next steep valley. By now they were many kilometres from the nearest road. Again they parked and searched.

The whole day passed; searching, returning to report, setting off again deeper into the forest. 'Don't give up!' Mandy urged. She knew that this would have to be their final attempt of the day. The light was fading from the lower slopes, the sun turning the sky a pale pink along the jagged horizon. Everyone got set for one last try. Gary went off with Mandy's mum, while Cherry and Mandy set out together. As usual, Katie searched alone.

Mandy led the way. She planned to follow a small stream; by now she was almost too tired to think. Her legs ached, her throat was dry and her damp hair stuck to her forehead and neck. But she vowed to look for the precious jarrah trees until she dropped.

They trudged deep into the valley in silence, Cherry following, looking sharply to left and right in the gathering gloom.

'Wait!' she said. She stopped in her tracks.

Mandy kept on walking, one foot after the other, on weary legs.

'Mandy, wait!' Cherry said again.

In a daze Mandy did as she was told. She half turned, saw Cherry staring through the dusk. Her arm was raised and stretched out, pointing across the stream. 'What is it?' She was so tired that she hardly dared hope.

'I'm not sure, but I think those are jarrahs!' Cherry stumbled down the steep gulley and splashed across the rocky bed of the stream.

Mandy followed. They scrambled up the far side, heaving themselves over the rocks, grabbing at ferns, reaching level ground. Then they were running across a small clearing, ignoring the kookaburras' angry cries, the crash and rustle of many small, darting animals who fled through the undergrowth. They stopped and stared up the massive smooth columns. Mandy knew they weren't eurabbies or peppermint-gums. They were the strong, straight trunks that she remembered from Glen Ives; tall and splendid. She turned to Cherry, unable to speak.

Cherry nodded. Her eyes closed and a smile spread across her tired face. 'Jarrahs!' she breathed. 'This is it, Mandy! We've found them!'

They rushed back to base to report the good news. Katie marked the map with a red star by the light of a torch, then she checked their bearings on the compass to make double-sure. With scarcely enough energy left to pitch tent, they crawled inside and slept.

Mandy woke to the high call of a dingo and a pale grey dawn. It was Sunday. Soon they were all wide awake, ready to race back in the Landcruiser to Blue Peak.

'We can leave the tents here until we come back,' Emily Hope suggested. 'It'll help keep us on the right track when we bring the koalas back with us.' She smiled brightly at Cherry and Mandy. 'I can't help thinking,' she murmured, 'that if it wasn't for you two we'd still be out there looking!'

Mandy agreed. 'It was Cherry who found the jarrahs!' she insisted.

Cherry blushed and pretended to be busy

packing up her sleeping-bag. 'It was a team effort,' she insisted.

'Well, anyway, well done.'

They set off for Blue Peak in high spirits. They would talk to Cherry's dad, Mike Macdonald, and ask him for any equipment he thought they might need to capture the koalas. Time was short, but now at least they'd found somewhere safe to bring the Glen Ives koalas. They'd done what everyone thought was impossible and found them a new home.

During the long drive they chatted about their rescue plan. The aim was to be in position at Glen Ives by mid-afternoon, complete with all they needed to transport the small colony of koalas back to Warragerri that night.

'It's going to be a long day, so get some rest,' Katie advised.

'We may find we have to sedate the koalas for the drive back,' Emily Hope said. 'They'll probably get worried about being taken away from the mountain.' She turned to Cherry. 'Will we be able to borrow some good strong cages from the animal sanctuary?' she asked.

Mandy listened to the careful preparations. She felt the warm breeze in her face as the Landcruiser made it to the nearest forest track and picked up speed. She trusted her mum's skill as a vet, and knew that from now on the jarrah koalas would get the very best care. She smiled happily at Gary. 'Was it worth missing a weekend's boogie boarding for? she asked.

'I reckon.' He nodded, fair hair blown back from his forehead, his arms slung along the back of his seat.

Mandy grinned at Cherry. The three of them sat back and relaxed as the car sped along, raising clouds of red dust on the dirt road.

They arrived at Blue Peak Wildlife Sanctuary just after lunch. The two rangers stepped out of the office on to the veranda. Mike raised his arm in greeting. 'Any luck?'

Mandy, Cherry and Gary stood up in the back of the open-topped car and yelled back. 'Yeah, we found some!' They jumped down as soon as Katie pulled into the yard. All three sprinted to share their news.

'Good on you!' Mike beamed back. He looked tired but satisfied. He shook Mandy and Gary by the hand and gave Cherry a big bear-hug. 'I hear you cracked the problem,' he said to Emily Hope and Katie as they approached.

Katie nodded. 'How about you? How did you get on?'

'We've been at it non-stop. We just brought eight more koalas on to the park. Five females, two babies, one boss male. We're going on to the reserve again now, to find them some nice new eurabbies. Then we reckon we've got two more trips up to Glen Ives before sundown. We aim to pick up eight or ten more on each trip, then we should be able to call it a day.'

'And with our colony of ten in the jarrah trees, you reckon that should be it? The bulldozers can move in tomorrow morning, no worries?' Katie sounded relieved.

'Well, we'll have done everything we can, let's just say that,' Mike agreed. His broad, sunburnt face turned serious. 'What do you say we grab a couple of big cages for you? They're round the back. Then we can all set off for Glen Ives together. I reckon we've still got our work cut out to clear the area before sundown. And I won't be happy until we've moved every last one!'

Spurred on by the ranger's urgent tone, they sprang into action. Miriam took Gary and Cherry round the back of the building, while Emily Hope reversed the Landcruiser into position, ready to stack the empty cages. Mike took Mandy and Katie to an inside storeroom, dark and musty.

'Let's hope you won't need these,' he muttered. He handed them coils of strong nylon rope and a couple of safety harnesses. 'With a bit of luck, your koalas will come along with you nice and easy, no worries. But just in case you need to climb up to bring a couple down, you'd better take these.'

They slung the ropes round their necks and grabbed a harness each. Mandy saw that even Katie looked worried.

'It won't come to that,' she whispered as they followed Mike back into the sunny yard.

'It might.' Mandy was prepared for anything.

'I've got all my fingers crossed – look!' Katie held up both hands.

'Why?'

'I can't stand heights, that's why,' she confessed.

Mandy felt her mouth drop open. 'You mean you're scared of them?' Until this moment she would have bet that their nurse didn't have a single weak spot.

'Scared to death.'

Mandy stared.

'OK, you follow us,' Mike ordered, taking charge.

They circled the yard and pointed out towards

the gate. Together the two rescue vehicles set off under the glare of the afternoon sun. Mandy felt the muscles in her stomach tighten, and she gripped the roll-bars as they came off-road across the steep hillside. Soon they cut across the old, narrow village road, within sight of the tiny church spire at the top of the hill. Then they dipped into forest once more. They headed quickly for the patch of doomed woodland.

Now all Mandy's thoughts were on the jarrah koalas. She hardly noticed the Sunday afternoon fossickers standing ankle-deep in the mountain stream. They bent double, sifting the pebbles for a sign of one tiny precious stone. She saw Mike draw to a halt up ahead and heard him give final instructions.

'This is where we split up,' he said. 'According to Cherry, your jarrahs are a click or so east of here. We head south-east to that patch of peppermints. OK?'

Emily Hope, who was at the wheel of the car, nodded. 'Is it a good idea for us to gather some jarrah leaves for the journey back to Warragerri?'

'If you can. But the main thing is to get as many of those koalas as you can safe inside those two cages before sundown,' he reminded them.

'*All* of them!' Mandy whispered to Gary and Cherry. 'We have to get all of them!'

Suddenly it didn't seem such an easy task. They split up from the two rangers and drove on towards the jarrah trees. At last they loomed ahead, tall and straight. But there wasn't a single koala in sight. They jumped from the car and stared up at the dizzy heights.

'I expect they're sleeping through this heat,' Mrs Hope said. She headed for the cool shade of a tall rock.

'Mum, hold it!' Mandy caught her arm. She remembered that the dark rock crevices were the favourite haunt of the king brown snake.

Gary jumped in with the offer of a piece of giant fern. 'Here, use this as a sunshade,' he advised. 'Keep to the open ground. You never know what you might find by those big rocks!' He winked at Mandy.

Emily Hope nodded and began to fan herself with the fern. Katie tilted her head back and turned full circle. 'Come on down, little koolewongs,' she begged. The sun pierced the shiny green leaves of the jarrah trees, speckling the ground with light and shade. 'We won't hurt you, just come on down!'

Mandy thought she saw a furry, grey-brown shape swing lazily through the highest branches. She could have been mistaken. Then she heard the grating cry. 'Awwgh! . . . Awwgh!' It sounded so far away, so high in the trees. 'Why don't they come down to see us?' she whispered to Cherry. Her neck was beginning to ache. Normally the koalas would spot them and come down in their friendly way, looking for treats. But today they stayed well hidden.

Cherry shook her head. 'I reckon they suspect something.'

'Awwgh! . . . Awwgh!' Another cry from another tree.

'They do sound different,' Mandy admitted. The dry, grating sound had an edge of fear that she'd never heard before. 'It's as if they don't trust us any more!'

'Would you?' Cherry frowned. 'They've probably caught on to the fact that Dad and Miriam are taking koalas out of the trees down there, putting them in cages and driving off with them. They've got it into their heads that we're up to no good.'

Mandy watched as another far-off shape swung itself higher up the trunk of the nearest jarrah, a mother with a baby clinging to her back. Mandy thought she spotted a quick look of fear as the mother moved out of danger. 'You can trust us!' she called softly, knowing that her words were useless.

Minutes ticked by. The jarrah trees grew still and silent. Mandy kept her eye on the mother koala who blinked warily down from a height of nine or ten metres. In the background they heard cries pierce the air as Mike succeeded in enticing yet another koala from its peppermint-gum tree into the strange, square space of a wooden cage with a grille, a lock, and no escape.

'Trust us!' Mandy pleaded. But the mother koala clung to her tree. She bunched her back legs beneath her, turned her face to one side. Her tufted ears blew slightly in the breeze. On her back the baby sat with his arms clasped round her neck. He looked down at the small band of rescuers. 'We've come to help!' she whispered.

But the Glen Ives koalas were scared. Something terrible was happening. Men had come to take them away from the safety of their homes. The forest was alive with the shrieks of cockatoos and kookaburras, as Mike and Miriam drove away with another colony of captive koalas. Sugar gliders floated across the blue gaps between the

eucalyptus trees. And all the time, Mandy heard the koalas' cry as they were driven off in their cages. Even in this heat, the sound chilled her.

'It sounds like a baby,' Mrs Hope sighed. 'Exactly like a human baby!'

They listened to the pitiful wails, and watched their own koalas retreat higher into the trees, further out of reach. Tomorrow the tree-fellers would come; the real menace.

Mandy closed her eyes and held her breath. Tomorrow would be too late. She pictured the whine of the buzz-saws, the violent swaying of branches, the tall trees crashing down. The trunks would topple, the defenceless jarrah-tree koalas would hurtle to their deaths.

Nine

Dusk drew in. Colour drained from the forest as the shadows lengthened. But still the colony of koalas stayed high in the jarrah trees.

'OK, that's it!' Emily Hope looked at her watch. 'If they won't come down, we'll have to go up!' She began to unbuckle one of the harnesses which Mike had given them.

'We could wait another fifteen minutes,' Katie suggested.

Mandy guessed the reason for her reluctance; Katie hated heights. She glanced from their nurse to her mum.

'No, by that time there won't be enough light

left to get up there and fetch them down.'

'But only two of us can go up.' Katie pointed to the two safety harnesses and the two coils of rope.

'Yes, and my guess is that if we can get hold of that mother and her baby and bring them down, the rest of the colony might well follow of their own accord. Mind you, we'll have to be very gentle.' Emily Hope stared up the long, straight trunk. 'Let's see how these contraptions work.' She slipped both arms inside the harness and began strapping herself securely in. 'Here's a clip to attach the rope to, I guess. Now, what should we do with the rope?'

Gary stepped forward with a practical suggestion. 'I reckon we sling it over a good, high branch. Then we wrap this free end around our waist. You're fastened tight to the other end, see. That way, if you fall, the rope tightens and the branch takes your weight. You're left swinging safe inside the harness!'

Mandy nodded. 'I get it!' She began to look out for the sturdiest branch. 'How about that one?'

Katie nodded and seized a rope. 'Here, let me have a go.' Expertly she threw one end high into the air. It snaked towards the branch, but fell just short. After two more attempts, Katie had slung the first rope securely round the tree. The second one was easier. She wrapped it round the branch at the first try.

They stood in a tight circle around the dangling ropes, waiting for the mother koala to settle back on to her branch. One or two other curious, blunt, furry faces peered down from nearby trees.

'Let me go up!' Mandy whispered. She wasn't in the least afraid of the climb, not with the rope and harness to save her if she fell. 'Please! I'm sure it's the same baby that I held before. He knows me. I think he'll come to me!'

Mrs Hope hesitated. It was a tricky climb.

'And I'm light!' Mandy insisted. 'It needs someone heavier to stay here on the ground to take my weight if I slip.'

'Let me go too!' Cherry jumped in. 'Mandy's right. We're the lightest, we should do the climbing while you three keep an eye on us from down here.'

'OK,' Mrs Hope said at last. She unstrapped the harness and handed it to Mandy. 'But be careful. No heroics once you're up there, remember. If the koalas refuse to come down, I don't want you taking any risks!' She looked straight into Mandy's eyes. 'Your dad would never forgive me!'

Mandy held her gaze. 'Don't worry, Mum. We'll be OK.'

Soon they were strapped in, the ropes were hooked into place by metal clips and they were ready to climb. Mrs Hope wound the free end of Mandy's rope two or three times around her own waist and planted her feet firmly on the ground. Katie did the same for Cherry, while Gary stood by to add his weight to either rope in case of emergency.

'Rather you than me,' he whispered to Mandy as she approached the giant tree. He gave her a leg up to the first branch.

'OK?' Mandy turned and asked Cherry. She felt calm, starting to plan a route from branch to branch, anxious now in case the mother and baby were afraid of the ropes and the climbing figures.

This was the time that koalas moved and fed; they were at their most alert. At the moment, the two koalas seemed to be looking on curiously at all this unusual activity. The wails of the other, captured koalas had faded, and their own colony had settled down again. Occasionally one called across the jarrahs, but there was no fresh panic as Emily Hope took the slack out of the rope and

Mandy began to move up the smooth trunk.

She climbed steadily from one low branch to another, finding footholds as she went. Below her, she could hear and feel Cherry following. Above, the mother koala shifted position. She let her legs dangle and straddle the branch, then she looked up towards the highest branches, ready to move on if necessary.

'Here!' Mandy called softly. She could see the pair of sturdy legs dangling and a curious face peering down.

'Awwgh!' The koala grumbled and shifted along the branch. Her baby gripped tight round her short neck and broad shoulders.

'Here, I won't harm you,' she promised. She glanced at the ground to judge her distance. They'd already climbed about six or seven metres. She saw her mum's upturned face, a pale oval full of concentration and concern. She gave her a thumbs-up and continued on her way.

'OK?' Cherry whispered. They edged upwards, heaving themselves from branch to branch, dizzy with the strong, sharp scent of eucalyptus.

'Fine!' Mandy looked for the next handhold. 'I think we must be nearly halfway!'

'One thing for sure,' Cherry gasped. They

paused again for breath. 'That mother and her baby can only go one way.'

'Up?'

She nodded. 'Worse luck!'

'Let's hope not,' Mandy whispered. Her hands were sore from grasping the tough bark and her legs and arms were scratched. But they were making good progress. 'Here,' she whispered in a soothing voice. 'Come down and say hello!'

But another koala set up a cry from a nearby tree. It sawed through the air, grating on their ears and alarming the mother and baby. The mother reached out her forelegs and sank her claws into the bark, then she pulled her hindlegs after her. She moved higher up the tree in a series of small hops.

Mandy groaned. Still the male koala cried out a warning.

'Listen!' Cherry let her rope take the strain and rested inside her harness. 'He must have heard Dad's car coming back!'

In the distance, Mandy heard the chug of an engine. It grew louder. Mike and his team were returning for their last bunch of koalas. All around, the branches of the jarrah trees shook and trembled as the whole colony reacted to the male's warning.

Mandy knew they were afraid again and moving up further out of reach. She clung to a branch and peered up after the mother and baby. Sure enough, they had disappeared from view.

'OK?' Emily called from below, her voice edged with tension.

'Fine!' Mandy repeated. She tried to sound more confident than she felt. 'You'll have to let out more rope. We've got to climb higher!' They'd reached a height of fifteen metres. The branches were slimmer, swaying gently in the breeze. The light was fading fast. At the last moment everything seemed to have gone wrong. But Mandy refused to give in.

She stepped up and put her foot on to the stump of a small branch. It cracked and broke under her weight. She clung on with both hands, feeling the jolt as her harness saved her.

'Mandy!' her mum cried out. Gary ran to help.

'It's OK. I'm not hurt. I'm going on up!' she insisted.

'Five more minutes!' Katie called. 'That's all the time we can risk. After that, you'll have to get yourselves back down here as quick as you can, koalas or no koalas!'

'OK,' Cherry agreed. 'Go ahead, Mandy; we can still do it!'

Mandy took a deep breath to steady her nerves. The broken branch was scary; how many more would give way and send shock waves through her whole body? Still, it was life and death for the koalas. She spotted two pairs of bright, shiny eyes, a hint of ash-grey fur, and once more she climbed towards them.

This time, curiosity seemed to overcome the mother. She stayed put as Mandy and Cherry drew near. She even paused to nibble at the tender new shoots on her branch. The baby shifted position to stare down at the girls.

Suddenly Mandy heard Cherry gasp. She felt her freeze. 'What is it?' she whispered.

'Nothing. I just looked down. I came over dizzy. I'm OK!' Cherry's voice sounded shaky and breathless.

Mandy's own mouth went dry. 'Sure?'

'Yes!'

'Listen, try not to look down again. You stay right there.' Without being able to see her friend's face, Mandy realised that Cherry couldn't go on. She knew that one more glance down into the shadowy depths would finish her off. 'You don't have to move for a while, OK? This branch won't take both our weights. I'm going to crawl out there and coax the baby away from his mother if I can. I'll try and bring him back to you and go back for the mother, OK?'

She set off without waiting for Cherry's answer, lying flat along the length of the thin branch and snaking her way forward. The wary mother had cornered herself at the furthest end of the branch. Soon Mandy was within actual reach.

She could see close-up the thick grey coat of the mother koala, the fluffy fawn fur of the baby. She could see the cheek pouches full of half-chewed leaves; she breathed in the powerful smell of cough sweets. She saw the mother's snout twitch and the baby swing one arm free. He stretched out his small black palm towards Mandy.

'Here!' she coaxed. 'Come and say hello.'

The baby let go of the mother and shuffled on to the branch. Mandy could almost touch him with her fingertips. He edged towards her, trusting this strange tree-climber. His mother rumbled a low warning, but she too seemed to think that Mandy was harmless. She watched as her baby sniffed at Mandy's fingers, shuffled further down the branch and into her arms.

Hardly daring to breathe, she cuddled the baby koala. She felt his soft, furry cheek against her face, his strong arm round her neck. Carefully she sat upright, edging backwards, legs astride the branch, back towards the main trunk. 'Cherry?' she whispered. 'Can you come and take him?'

Cherry forced herself into action. She stretched out both arms, ready to take the half-grown koala. He nuzzled Mandy's cheek, then agreed to depart. Soon he was nestled safely in Cherry's arms and his mother was ambling along the branch after him. Mandy reached out and scratched her head. 'You're a good mother,' she murmured. 'Come on, girl, let's go down and see the others.'

Cherry had begun the long descent, planting her feet against the main trunk and letting the rope take the strain. She held on to the baby and abseiled down, watched from below by an anxious Mrs Hope, Katie and Gary.

'Let's go!' Mandy said again. She knew the mother would be too heavy to manage easily. She hoped she would make her own way down. The koala blinked and sighed at all the excitement. Then she swung easily on to the trunk, past Mandy, gripping with all fours. She didn't need ropes and harness as she went ahead, following her baby to the ground.

Gary stood ready with handfuls of tender green

shoots, Katie unclipped Cherry's harness and flung both arms around her and the baby koala. Emily gently lifted the mother down the last metre or so, her own eyes flooded with relief as Mandy finally made it to the ground.

Mandy felt the earth under her feet. They'd done it! They'd saved at least two of the koalas. She stood in the darkening forest, her legs shaking, her chest heaving after the strenuous climb. Now she heard other koalas calling, other furry shapes swinging through the branches, down the trunks, shuffling along the ground to investigate their strange, unexpected visitors.

Ten

The koalas wailed and cried as Mandy and her friends put them gently into the cages in the back of the Landcruiser.

The whole colony had gathered round the first mother and her lively baby, slowly gaining confidence as Cherry crouched to make inviting noises and to offer them delicious sprigs of jarrah. First the big, noisy boss male came down from his tree. He blundered towards the group, snatched greedily at the leaves and stuffed them into his mouth. His cheeks puffed out as he grunted and chewed. Then the second male followed, steering well clear of the boss. He took food from Gary and squatted on his haunches, picking at the leaves with delicate fingers.

The females came down together, all four from a different direction, three with babies clinging to them. Then another baby, only a few weeks old, scarcely covered in fur, its eyes still half shut, appeared nose-first. He crawled slowly out of the pouch on to his mother's back.

'A new baby!' Mandy whispered. The mother was happy for her to scoop him into her cupped palm. The tiny creature licked her palm. He nuzzled for food, so she put him back on the mother's chest. He fumbled and turned, sought out the pouch and disappeared.

Mandy beamed at her mum. By now all the jarrah koalas had gathered in a contented group. She counted. There were ten. She added one extra; the young baby.

'It looks like they're all here,' Katie said. 'Now listen, luckily for us these chaps don't move around too quick. I reckon we can take the five females with their babies all in one go, pop them into the cages, and shoot back for the two males before they have time to get very far. OK?'

They nodded. This was the part that Mandy knew she wouldn't enjoy. She reminded herself that it was for the koalas' own good, and tried to shut her ears to the pitiful noises.

It was hard. They cried like little children as they were lifted into the clean, wire-fronted cages. The babies clung to their mothers, small faces crumpled with distress, mouths open, wailing. Emily Hope and Katie left the three kids in charge of the captives and set off after the two males. The boss had lumbered to the base of his tree, but Mrs Hope easily held him and brought him back. Katie headed off the second male and tackled him from the side. He rolled over, soft as a teddy bear, then waited to be picked up.

In spite of the cries from inside the cages, Mandy smiled. 'Poor old things. They haven't a clue! No wonder they can't look after themselves if they just roll over and give up!'

Soon every single one was inside the cages, complete with a heap of freshly picked leaves. Mrs Hope gave them a quick once-over. 'OK, they look pretty fit and healthy,' she decided. 'They should all survive the journey. Let's go.'

Katie was at the wheel. Gary sat alongside, while Cherry, Mandy and her mum squashed in the back beside the captive koalas. Mandy felt a surge of relief as the engine roared into life. They would

drive through the darkness, hoping to arrive at Warragerri before first light.

They made only one stop, at the office in Blue Peak. Katie drew up and jumped down into the yard. She strode up the steps. From the car they could hear her telling Miriam that they'd gathered up all eleven of the jarrah koalas.

Mandy heaved a deep sigh. 'Can I shoot in and give dad a ring?' she asked her mum. 'I'm sure he'd want to know.'

Mrs Hope nodded. 'Quick as you can.'

Mandy dashed inside and rang the Mitchell Gap number. By now it was quite late. She looked at her watch; it was half-past ten. She waited what seemed like an age before someone picked up the phone. 'Hi, Dad. It's me. We did it. We found the jarrah trees! We've been to collect the koalas from Glen Ives. Now we're going to set them free on Warragerri!'

'Whoa!' Adam Hope laughed down the phone. 'Mandy, that's fantastic! When?' He sounded a long way away.

'At dawn tomorrow. Mum says that's the best time. Katie thinks we should just about make it.'

'No worries,' he assured her. 'Listen, when will you and your mum be home?'

'Later tomorrow.' She paused.

'Good. I've missed you,' he said simply and cheerfully. 'Hey, listen, I saw the platypus in the creek with her babies.'

'When?'

'This morning. She's quite a sight.'

'Great.' Mandy felt a sudden pang of home-sickness for Mitchell Gap. 'Right, Dad, I'd better be off.'

'Rightio. I'll be thinking of you! Safe journey, love.'

'Thanks, Dad.'

'Take care,' he said gently before he put down the receiver.

She sighed again and dashed back out to the car. Cherry had left a message with Miriam that she was driving to Warragerri to help set the koalas free. 'I wouldn't miss it for the world!' she vowed.

'Me neither,' Gary agreed. He kept careful guard over the cages, shooing off a curious dingo that loped across the dark yard.

'Hold tight!' Katie ordered. She turned the car round. The headlights raked across the empty yard. 'This is going to be a tough ride!' They were wide awake, high on a wave of success as they rode out into the night.

* * *

Dawn rose pearly grey. There was a white mist on the upper slopes of Mount Warragerri. A mob of kangaroos loped steadily downhill into the warmer valley, ignoring the red Landcruiser as Katie parked it quietly by the stream. Mandy had spotted their two tents, covered in dew. Great drops had gathered on the fly-sheets and dripped to the ground.

'Here we are!' she whispered. Her eyes felt raw and prickly after a night without sleep, but she was fully alert to every sight and sound.

'This is as far as we can get in the car,' Mrs Hope said. 'We'll have to carry the cages from here, across country to the jarrahs.'

'How far is it?' Katie asked. Gently they lifted the cages to the ground. Inside, the nervous koalas huddled together.

'About ten minutes, I reckon.' Cherry pointed in the right direction, sure of her way.

'Right. You lead. The rest of us will carry the cages. We might have to stop for rests,' Mrs Hope warned. 'On the other hand, we want to get a move on. The sun will soon be up, and we want to see these little honeys safe and sound in their new home before then!'

Mandy took hold of her end of one of the heavy cages with a strange flutter of mixed feelings. Like her mum, she was eager to see the koalas safely back into the wild. This was what they'd worked for, slogging up the mountains, climbing the dizzy height of the Glen Ives jarrah. But she had learned to love these beautiful, gentle creatures and would hate to see them go.

It was true what people said about them, that they were some of the friendliest and most loveable creatures in the world. Mandy's heart melted just to look at them. But she must let go of them, she knew that. She walked quietly ahead of Katie, who carried the other end of the cage.

In five minutes they would open the door and lift the first koala to freedom. It would break Mandy's heart and she would be overjoyed, both at the same time. Then she would go home and probably never see them again. Life was strange. She plodded on through the forest, arms aching with the weight of the koalas.

It was a bitter-sweet dawn. Cherry, their expert guide, led them straight to the jarrah trees. They soared overhead under a sky tinged with pink. Birds flew, bright flashes of orange, red and blue.

'OK?' Katie whispered.

Mandy unlocked the first cage. She lifted her favourite baby into her arms. 'Come with me.'

She turned to walk to the nearest tree, hearing the mother koala clamber out of the cage and follow close behind. 'Here you are,' she said without fuss. She put the baby on to the ground and stepped back. Her arms felt suddenly empty.

The baby waited for his mother and climbed on to her back. His little, thin-lipped slit of a mouth seemed to stretch into a smile. Then mother and baby slowly climbed the tree trunk, out of reach, higher and higher, scenting the jarrah leaves, looking eagerly ahead.

She stood and watched as other koalas followed; three, four, five. The boss male lumbered towards a new tree, his cry grating through the air.

'Did you know, koalas have the loudest voice in Australia?' Katie asked. She watched, head back, arms folded.

'Awwgh! Awwgh!' The boss male jumped lazily up his very own tree.

Mandy smiled at Cherry and Gary. 'We believe it!' she said. Six, seven, eight, nine, ten, eleven. She counted them all safely out of sight.

They vanished into the high treetops. As the sun rose, there was no sign of the koalas except for that extraordinary, childlike cry.

'Come on. Time to go home,' Emily Hope said quietly. She put her arm round Mandy's shoulder and walked her slowly back to the car.

Home to Mitchell Gap and Hilda Harris's tom-cat. Home to her dad, while the jarrah-tree koalas blinked sleepily at the rising sun and settled in for a good day's sleep in their new home at Warragerri.

That night, safe in her own room, Mandy dreamed of her baby koala. He perched on the end of her bed, fat and happy, slowly chewing, smiling through it all. She woke up the next morning, ready for whatever the day would bring.

Dear Reader,

*I'm so pleased with the letters I have been receiving about **Animal Ark**. It seems there are a great number of fans of the series, and I am very happy that so many people are enjoying the books.*

I especially enjoy reading your suggestions for new titles – so keep them coming!

Much love

Lucy Daniels

RSPCA

Join the Animal Action Club!

If you like *Animal Ark*® then you'll love the RSPCA's Animal Action Club! Anyone under 13 can become a member for just **£8** a year. Join up and you can look forward to six issues of *Animal Action* magazine – each one is bursting with news, competitions, features, celebrity interviews and a great poster! Plus we'll send you a fab joining pack and a **FREE** RSPCA *Perfect Pets* cuddly toy (worth £4.99) too!!

To join, simply complete the form below – a photocopy is fine – and send it with a cheque for £8 (made payable to RSPCA) to RSPCA Animal Action Club, Wilberforce Way, Southwater, Horsham, West Sussex RH13 9RS. We'll then send your joining pack, free toy and first issue of *Animal Action*.

Don't delay, join today!

Name:

Address:

Postcode:	Date of birth:

Signature of parent/guardian:

Data Protection Act: This information will be held on computer and used only by the RSPCA.

Please note: we cannot guarantee the type of soft toy you will receive and please allow 28 days for delivery. **AACHOD04**